Dedication

In Memory Of my children Alexis and Ja'Colby

Momma did this for you both, and with you watching over me, I'll do more. Caleb "Jugg" Martin, Josiah "Phatt" Sanderson, Desmond "Lil' Des" Cook, Jaeshaun "Solo Jae" Pleasure, Stephanie "Stank" Hardin, Gregory "G-Jamm" McLin, Mykus "Higgo" Higgins, Rashad "Bruce" Moody, Cameron "Cam" Turner, Braylin "Bray" Jones, My Tat2 and Yoneko, Cedric "Mann" Jackson, Rayshaun "Ray" Bates

Dedicated to
My children Victoria and Miracle, my grandkids, my husband, my parents, my siblings, and everyone that believed in me.

Mildred "Memaw" Malone; I Love You!

URBAN RISE
A Story of Struggle, Ambition, and Survival

Shunetta R Garth-Owens

Table of Contents

Chapter One
Concrete Beginnings

Alexis Grant learned early that the world didn't wait for little girls to catch up. At nine years old, she already knew how to mix a bottle for her baby sister, how to hush her brothers when gunshots popped too close, and how to read her mother's mood by the way she entered a room.

Her building on the south side leaned like it was tired of standing, graffiti climbing its walls like vines. Police sirens were the neighborhood lullaby. Her mother, Serena, drifted in and out of the apartment; sometimes smiling too wide, sometimes crying too hard, sometimes disappearing for days. And her father, Rico… well, he was a businessman of the street. Women came and went under his orders. Everyone in the neighborhood knew what he did, but nobody said it out loud; not if they wanted to keep their teeth.

Alexis, the oldest of four, became the glue holding the family together. She'd wake before dawn, braid her sister Mia's hair, tie her brothers' shoes, and walk them all to school with her chin lifted like she wasn't carrying the weight of a world no kid should have to carry.

But Alexis was different from the block. She felt it. Every time she looked out from the cracked balcony at the skyline, the sharp steel angles of the city, shining even from miles away, she felt something shift in her chest.

One day, she told herself that's where I'm going. Past the corner boys, past the sirens, past the invisible cage people said she'd never escape.

She kept a notebook hidden in her backpack; pages filled with drawings of buildings, sketches inspired by pictures she stole from the school library. Architectural dreams. She didn't tell her soul. Dreams were fragile things here, people crushed them without thinking.

At fourteen, when most kids worried about popularity or phones they couldn't afford, Alexis worried about rent, about groceries, and about whether her mother would survive the night, but she studied Hard.

And she worked; bagging groceries, cleaning apartments, and tutoring kids who needed help reading. Every dollar went into a jar she hid under a floorboard. She called it her "escape fund." In her mind, she could already see a future where she owned her own business, her own home, something no one could take from her.

People on the block would watch her pass and whisper, "That girl's going somewhere." They were right. Alexis wasn't just surviving. She was sharpening herself, grit against circumstance, disciplined against chaos. And someday soon, she'd rise from the very concrete that tried to hold her down.

Chapter Two
Lessons from the Block

By the time Alexis hit fifteen, she had mastered the art of disappearing. Not physically, everyone on the block knew her. But she had learned how to make herself small when her father stomped into the apartment angry, or when her mother came home shaking, eyes glassy and unfocused. She blended into corners, kept her siblings quiet, and made herself a ghost in her own home.

But at school?

She refused to be invisible.

Alexis sat in the front row of every class, absorbing knowledge like warmth on a freezing day. Teachers noticed her dedication; how she copied notes twice to memorize them, how she stayed after school for extra help even when she needed to rush home and cook for her siblings.

One teacher in particular, Ms. Rivera, kept an eye on her. She was young, fresh out of college, still believing she could save kids one life at a time.

One afternoon, Ms. Rivera stopped her after class.

"Alexis, you ever think about college?"

Alexis blinked. College felt like a foreign word; something rich kids talked about, something she only saw in movies.

"I think about surviving," she said honestly. Ms. Rivera didn't flinch. "You can do both."

Alexis wanted to laugh, but something in the teacher's eyes, steady, certainly made her pause.

"You have talent," Ms. Rivera continued, pulling out a folder. Inside were sketches Alexis didn't even remember handing them in. "Real talent. You ever consider, architecture?"

Alexis froze. Her throat tightened. How did she know?

The notebook hidden in her floorboard suddenly felt like it weighed a hundred pounds.

Ms. Rivera smiled, gentle but unshakeable. "I know that look. I had dreams once too. Alexis swallowed. "Dreams don't mean much around my way." "Then let's change your way."

It was the first time an adult spoke to her like she was capable of more than holding a broken home together.

But reality didn't wait for her to finish daydreaming.

That night, the chaos in the Grant apartment swelled like a storm.

Her father came home angry about money being missing, and one of his girls ran off.

Doors slammed. Voices rose. Serena cried. Her father shouted at her in silence.

Alexis pushed her siblings into the bedroom, closing the door behind them.

"Read to them," she whispered to her brother Jalen. "Loud enough to block the noise."

Jalen nodded, pulling out a wrinkled picture book with shaking hands.

Alexis crept into the hallway where her parents' fight echoed. She saw her father pacing, chest heaving, knuckles bruised. Her mother curled on the couch, tears streaking her face.

"You think you can just disappear on me?" Rico barked. "You think I don't know where you been?"

Serena whispered something, but Alexis couldn't hear the words. Her father's hand was lifted.

Without thinking, Alexis moved.

"Stop."

Her voice cut through the room like a blade.

Rico turned, eyes narrowing. "What you say?"

Alexis didn't back down. She couldn't. Not with her mother trembling. Not with her siblings in the next room listening.

"Leave her alone," she said. Her voice wasn't loud. But it was steady.

Rico stepped towards her. He was intimidating; lean, sharp, dangerous. The kind of man people crossed the street to avoid.

"You grown now?" he asked. "You think you run this house?"

Alexis's heart pounded so hard she felt sick. But she kept her chin up.

"I run what you can't," she said quietly. "The kids. The bills. Everything you forget when you're out there."

A long, tense silence stretched between them. Then Rico laughed; short, humorless.

"You just like your mother," he hissed. "Think a strong voice makes you strong."

He shoved past her and stormed out, slamming the door behind him.

Serena sobbed into her hands.

Alexis stood still until she stopped shaking.

Then she walked to the window, staring out at the city lights. Each sparkle on the skyline felt like a promise.

I'm getting out, she told herself.

And I'm taking them with me.

She didn't know how yet.

But the streets had taught her something important: Every empire starts with a single, stubborn dream.

Chapter Three
Hustle Money

Two weeks after the blow-up with her father, Alexis made a decision. If she was going to get out, she needed money, no pocket change from grocery bags and apartment cleaning. Real money. Enough to move her and her siblings somewhere safe. Enough to build a different life.

Her escape fund jar had only two hundred and thirteen crumpled dollars. It felt like nothing. Like trying to climb a skyscraper with a broken ladder.

But Alexis had something the streets respected: hustle. So, she started getting creative. Every morning before school, she hustled breakfast sandwiches outside the bus stop. Bread, eggs, cheese simple. She bought ingredients with grocery coupons and stayed up before sunrise cooking. Kids on the block loved them. Teachers started buying them too.

At school, she sold sketches; portraits, graffiti-style names, tattoo designs. Five dollars here, ten dollars there. Her talent spread fast.

By the time she walked home each day, her backpack jingled with coins and small bills.

But hustle alone didn't make life easier.

Her father's anger simmered since their confrontation. He came home less, but when he did, he'd stare at her too long, like he was trying to figure out who she was becoming; and whether that threatened him.

Serena grew quieter, disappearing into her room for hours, sometimes days, coming out with slurred apologies and promises she couldn't keep.

Alexis stayed busy, kept her siblings fed, clothed, protected. She controlled what she could and ignored what she couldn't.

But the world had a way of testing you when you least expected it.

One Friday evening, on her way home from work at the corner store, Alexis heard someone call her name.

"Lex!"

She turned to see Devin; one of the older boys from the block; leaning against a streetlight. He was twenty, maybe, lean and sharp-eyed, a hustler but not the dangerous kind. He always treated her with respect.

"You been moving' different lately," he said, walking up. Alexis sighed. "Just busy."

"I see that." He nodded toward the small grocery bag in her hand. "You are watching out for the kids again?"

"Always."

Devin pulled a small wad of bills from his pocket. "I got something for you." Alexis froze. "I'm not taking your money."

"It isn't charity." He smirked. "I want a design. For a tattoo." She blinked. "A tattoo?"

"Yeah. Something clean. Something that looks like… I don't know. A new start."

That hit her harder than she expected.

"A new start," she repeated softly.

Devin shrugged. "You're good at that drawing stuff. Figure I might as well go to the best."

Alexis tried not to smile. "Twenty bucks." "Bet."

He handed her the cash. Real cash. Not sweaty lunch money or crumpled coins. It felt heavy in her hand. Respect heavy.

"What you want it to say?" she asked.

Devin looked at her for a long moment before answering.

"'Rise.'"

Her breath caught. It was simple, but powerful. Like someone had looked straight into her chest and pulled out the word she lived by.

She nodded. "I'll draw it."

And that's how it started, her unofficial side hustle as the block's designer. Word spread. People wanted tattoos, album covers, murals, logos. She charged modestly at first, then more when demand grew.

The jar under her floorboard started filling faster. Three hundred dollars.

Four hundred.

Six hundred.

Enough to make the dream feel a little less distant.

But one night, everything almost shattered.

She came home late from a drawing session at Devin's place and found her father sitting at the kitchen table, counting money. The room stank of smoke and cheap cologne.

He didn't look up when she walked in.

"Where you are getting' all this cash?" he asked casually, too casually.

Alexis's chest tightened. She hadn't told him anything. She didn't trust him with a penny.

"I work," she said carefully.

Rico chuckled. "Kids don't make money like that."

She stayed silent.

He finally lifted his eyes; dark, sharp, calculating.

"You aren't running' something behind my back, are you? Cause if you are…" He tapped the table with one thick finger. "We got a problem."

Alexis felt the weight of her future; her siblings' future; rest on her next words.

8

"No," she said. "I'm just drawing for people."

Rico stared at her. Long enough to make her palms sweat.

Then he laughed again, softer this time. "As long as you aren't messing with my business."

Her jaw clenched. His business. The one that ruined lives, destroyed families, took her mother from her piece by piece.

She nodded, because disagreeing was dangerous. He went back to his money.

But Alexis's decision hardened like steel inside her. She wasn't just trying to escape anymore.

She was planning it.

And the day she left, she'd make sure her father would never hurt her family again.

Chapter Four
Cracks in the Concrete

Autumn hit the city hard that year.

Cold winds scraped between buildings, rattling windows and chilling bones. Alexis wrapped her siblings in extra layers each morning before school. She patched hand-me-downs, tightened shoelaces, checked homework, and counted the money in her escape jar every night like a ritual.

Seven hundred and forty-two dollars. Still not enough.

But it was something.

She was building something.

One Thursday afternoon, Ms. Rivera pulled her aside after class.

"You've been quiet lately," she said gently. "More than usual." Alexis shrugged. "Just tired."

"Alexis... you don't have to do everything alone."

That sentence landed like a bruise. True, but impossible.

Ms. Rivera hesitated, then reached into her desk drawer and handed her a brochure.

"Next month, the city's youth arts competition opens. Winner gets a scholarship and a mentorship with a major architecture firm."

Alexis stared at the glossy paper. The bold text. The images of models and blueprints. A world she wanted so badly it hurt.

"I can't," she whispered. "Why not?"

"I don't have time for competitions. I'm working. I'm taking care of;"

"Your family," Ms. Rivera finished softly. "I know. But your future matters too."

Alexis didn't reply. The idea of choosing herself felt selfish. Dangerous. Impossible.

But she tucked the brochure into her bag anyway.

That night, the apartment felt wrong the moment she stepped inside. Too quiet. Too still.

The TV was on, but it was just static, hissing into the empty living room.

"Mama?" she called.

No answer.

"Mia? Jalen? Ty?"

Silence.

A cold dread slid down her spine.

She checked the bedrooms, her heart pounding until her ribs hurt; empty.

empty. empty.

Panic clawed at her throat.

She ran outside onto the balcony, scanning the street below. Then she heard soft crying, coming from the stairwell.

She sprinted to it, nearly tripping over her own feet.

Her siblings were huddled on the landing; Mia holding Ty, Jalen pressing a hand to his cheek, trying not to cry.

"Baby, what happened?" Alexis dropped to her knees.

"It; it was Dad," Jalen whispered. "He was mad. He said the house wasn't clean. even though we cleaned it. He said, he said we were getting in his way."

Alexis pulled them all close. Rage simmered inside her, hotter than anything she'd ever felt. Her father hadn't laid a hand on her siblings in years; not since she learned to throw herself between them.

But he'd done it tonight. When she wasn't home. "Where is he?" she asked, voice tight.

"Left," Mia sniffed. "He left after he yelled." "And Mama?"

Jalen shook his head. "We don't know. She wasn't awake."

Alexis swallowed hard.

This was the breaking point.

The line between surviving and choosing something different.

She stood. "We're going upstairs. Pack a bag. Only what you need."

The kids froze.

"Are we… leaving?" Mia whispered. "Not yet," Alexis said. "But soon."

They slept together in her bed that night; four bodies tucked under one blanket, listening for footsteps, for danger, for anything.

Alexis didn't sleep at all.

She stared at the ceiling, thinking of the competition brochure in her backpack. The scholarship. The chance. The way Ms. Rivera said, "your future matters too." Her siblings' soft breathing filled the room.

She thought about the money in the jar. The bruises on Jalen's cheek. Her mother wasting away.

And she made a decision.

She wasn't waiting anymore.

If the streets wanted to break her, they'd have to try harder.

Tomorrow, she will enter that competition.

Tomorrow, she will take the first step out of the life she was born into. And she would drag her family out   one way or another.

Chapter Five
The Blueprint of Dreams

Alexis arrived at school the next morning with her mind already set. No hesitation. No second thoughts.

She was entering the competition.

The hallway buzzed with noise; kids talking loud, lockers slamming, sneakers squeaking across tile; but she walked through it all with tunnel vision. Her life had always been divided in two:

The world she had.

And the world she wanted. Today, she was bridging the gap.

During lunch, she found Ms. Rivera in her classroom, grading papers with a half-eaten salad on her desk.

"I'm doing it," Alexis said, holding the brochure. "I'm entering."

Ms. Rivera looked up, and in her expression was something Alexis rarely saw from adults: pride that didn't expect anything in return. "Good," she said warmly. "Then let's get to work."

She cleared a space on her desk and pulled out a stack of drawing paper, rulers, pencils, and an architectural template.

"First step," she said, "we need a concept. A structure that represents you."

Alexis hesitated. Buildings were more than shapes to her, they were symbols of escape, strength, freedom. She thought of nights on cracked balconies, staring at city lights. Of the skyline that promised more than the block ever could.

"I want to design something... strong," she said slowly. "For people who start with nothing. Something that feels safe."

Ms. Rivera nodded. "Then sketch from that place."

Alexis inhaled, exhaled, and began drawing.

Her pencil moved like it already knew the way. A foundation. Support beams. Curved walls that embraced the center. A rooftop garden. Sunlight windows. A design bold enough to stand out, real enough to build.

When she finished the rough outline, Ms. Rivera's eyebrows lifted. "Alexis... this is extraordinary."

For the first time, Alexis didn't shrug it off.

She knew it too.

She spent the next two weeks pouring every extra minute between work, chores, and taking care of her siblings, perfecting her design.

On the phone, Devin offered his apartment as a quiet workspace.

"You need somewhere your pops won't bother you," he said. "I got you."

She accepted. Not because she trusted easily, but because she needed help, and Devin had proven he wasn't the type to ask for anything back that she wasn't willing to

14

give.

Night after night, she worked at his little kitchen table while he played soft music in the background, sometimes sketching his own tattoo ideas, sometimes talking about life on the block and how he wanted out too.

It was the closest thing Alexis had to peace.

But peace never lasted long in her world.

One night, as she walked home with her portfolio tucked safely under her arm, she noticed a familiar car parked outside her building.

Her father's.

Her stomach dropped.

The lights in the apartment were on; and she could hear yelling from outside. Her mother's voice. Her father's. The thud of something hitting the wall.

Alexis froze. Not again.

Not tonight.

Not when she was so close to changing everything.

She ran upstairs, pushed the door open, and stepped inside.

Her father was in the middle of the living room, pacing like a caged animal. Serena sat on the couch, crying. The kids huddled near the hallway, too scared to move.

Rico turned when he heard the door.

"Where you been?" he snapped. Alexis held her ground. "School."

"You always 'at school.'" His lips curled. "You think I don't know what you're doing? Running off to some boy's place? Getting smart with me?"

She swallowed hard. "I'm working on something. Something important." "You mean this?" He grabbed something off the table.

Her portfolio.

Her heart stopped.

"Where did you get that?" she demanded.

"Found it," he said, smirking. "Looked inside." Alexis's pulse thundered. "Give it back."

Rico flipped through her architectural drawings like they were trash mail. "You think you special or something? You think you are better than me? Better than this family?"

The room tightened around her. Her siblings held their breath. Her mother shook her head weakly, terrified.

Alexis stepped forward. "Give. It. Back."

Her father laughed.

And tore one of her pages in half.

15

The sound; soft, ripping paper; hit her harder than any punch. Her future, torn in his hands.

Something inside her snapped.

She didn't shout. She didn't cry.

She just stared at him, cold and still.

"You don't own me," she said quietly.

Her father froze. "What you say?" "You heard me."

Rico's jaw clenched, and for a moment, Alexis saw violence flash in his eyes.

But before he could step toward her, Jalen ran between them.

"Leave her alone!" he cried.

The moment shattered like glass. Her father hesitated, thrown off. Alexis scooped up her siblings, grabbed what was left of her portfolio, and backed toward the door.

"We're leaving," she said.

"You walk out that door," Rico growled, "and don't come back."

Alexis stared at him dead in the eyes.

"That's the idea."

She walked out with her siblings behind her, leaving the door open, not out of carelessness, but defiance.

Tonight, the concrete cracked.

And through the cracks, something fierce was growing. Not just survival.

A future.

Chapter Six
Shelter and Resolve

The hallway was cold, dim, and silent except for the sound of four pairs of hurried footsteps. Alexis kept her siblings close; her torn portfolio clutched under her arm like a wounded limb.

"Where are we going?" Mia whispered, shivering in her thin jacket.

Alexis didn't know; not exactly. But she knew where they couldn't go back inside that apartment.

"Somewhere safe," she said. "I promise."

She led them down the stairs, out of the building, and into the sharp night air. The streetlamps flickered weakly above them. Cars passed without slowing. It was the kind of night where people looked the other way on purpose.

Ty rubbed his eyes sleepily. Jalen kept touching the bruise on his cheek, absently, like he wanted to rub the memory away. Mia carried her backpack with both arms, like she thought someone might try to take it.

Alexis pulled out her cracked phone and made the only call she could think of.

Devin answered on the third ring. "Lex? You good?"

"No." Her voice wavered despite her best effort. "We need somewhere to go. For tonight. Just one night."

"Say less," he said immediately. "Come over."

Devin lived three blocks away, in an old building with crooked stairs and too many locks on the door. But inside, it was warm, clean, and safe; three luxuries Alexis. didn't take lightly.

He opened the door wide when he saw them. "Damn... y'all okay?" "No," Jalen said bluntly.

Devin didn't ask more. He just stepped aside and let them in.

While Mia and the boys settled onto the couch with blankets, Alexis stood near the door, portfolio pressed to her chest.

Devin nodded at it. "He messed it up?"

Alexis slowly opened it.

Half the pages were bent. Some were torn. Pencil lines smudged. Hours and hours of work damaged. Not destroyed but wounded. Like her.

She tried to blink back the heat in her eyes.

"It's fine," she lied.

Devin shook his head. "Nah. That aren't fine. That's your shot right there." Alexis clenched her jaw. "I'll redraw it. Every page. I'll fix it."

He watched her for a moment, quiet, then said, "You don't have to act strong in front of me, you know."

"I'm not acting," she said.

18

She was too used to holding the world on her shoulders to put it down now.

Later that night, when her siblings finally fell asleep on a pile of worn blankets, Devin handed her a steaming mug of tea.

"You staying here till you figure something out," he said. "No arguing." Alexis sighed. "This is temporary, Dev."

"I know." He leaned against the wall. "But you got to breathe somewhere."

She didn't answer. Instead, she pulled out her ruined drawings and spread them across the small kitchen table. Even though they were torn, they looked like something, like ambition, like possibility.

She picked up a pencil.

Devin raised an eyebrow. "You are drawing right now?"

"I don't have time to waste," she murmured. "The competition's in a week. I need to redo everything."

He glanced at the clock. "It's almost midnight."

"Then I better start."

And she did.

Pencil strokes filled the quiet apartment. Soft graphite against paper. The sound of rebuilding.

Line by line, page by page, she recreated what her father tried to destroy. And this time, the lines were sharper. The buildings are stronger. The vision more defiant.

Each sketch carried the weight of her siblings' soft breathing in the next room. Each measurement felt like a promise.

Devin stayed up too, even though he didn't need to; sometimes sketching beside. her, sometimes just watching, making sure she didn't fall asleep at her work. "You ever going to give yourself a break?" he asked at one point.

"When I win," she said simply.

By sunrise, a faint orange glow filled the window. The city felt quieter, softer, like the world was giving her a moment of mercy.

Alexis stretched, exhausted but proud. She had redrawn half the project. Her fingers ached. Her back hurt.

But her spirit? Untouched.

Unbroken.

Mia woke first, rubbing her eyes and sitting up.

"Lex... are we going home today?"

Alexis looked at her little sister, hair messy, cheeks puffy from sleep, eyes too old for her age.

"No," she said softly. "Not yet."

"Okay," Mia whispered, trusting her completely.

That single word, that trust, hardened Alexis's resolve into something unshakable.

The shelter was temporary. The fear was temporary.

The struggle was temporary.

But what she was building, her future, was permanent.

And no one, not even her father, was ever going to take it from her again.

Chapter Seven
Shadows on the Block

For the next three days, Devin's small apartment became command central.

Alexis woke before dawn, helped her siblings wash and dress, dropped them at school, worked a shift at the corner store, picked the kids up, fed them, then sketched until her fingers cramped.

By the fourth night, her architectural model was almost ready; clean lines, sharp. angles, the blueprint of a life she hadn't lived yet but believed in with every breath.

Everything was coming together. But the block was watching.

And whispers travel fast in the streets.

The trouble arrived quietly at first.

A woman from Rico's circle; Shawna, one of his "employees"; spotted Alexis outside the bodega.

"Your dad been looking' for you," she said, chewing gum loud. "Real mad." Alexis's stomach twisted, but she didn't flinch. "That's his problem."

Shawna smirked. "You talk tough now you are staying' with that boy?"

Heat rose in Alexis's chest, but she kept her voice steady. "Mind your business."

Shawna held up both hands. "Just saying'. Rico isn't the type to let disrespect slide."

Alexis turned away before Shawna could see her fear.

She'd made her choice when she walked out that door.

But choices had consequences.

That night, after the kids were asleep and Devin was sketching designs on the couch, Alexis sat at the kitchen table staring at her half-finished architectural model.

Her hands shook, just a little.

"You, okay?" Devin asked quietly.

"No," she admitted. "He's looking for me."

Devin nodded slowly. "He isn't getting near you. I won't let that happen." "You can't fight him," she said. "You know that."

He looked down at his sketchbook. "Maybe not. But I'm not letting him touch you or your siblings."

Something warm flickered in her chest, something she didn't have time to name.

"I can handle him," she said. "I just have to survive until the competition. Then… maybe I'll have a real shot."

"A real shot at what?"

"Leaving," she whispered. "For good." Devin didn't answer.

He didn't need to.

They both knew escape wasn't simple on the block.

Not when people like her father survived by control.

But they also both knew she wasn't backing down.

Two days before the competition, the danger finally showed its teeth.

Alexis was walking home with her siblings when a black car rolled slowly beside them.

Her heart dropped.

The passenger window lowered.

Rico's voice drifted out, smooth and venomous. "Get in the car, Alexis."

Mia gripped her hand so tight it hurt. Jalen stepped in front of Ty instinctively.

Alexis didn't stop walking.

"I said get in the car," Rico repeated, louder.

She kept moving.

Her pulse hammered. The kids clung to her. The street felt too empty, too exposed.

Rico pushed the door open and stepped out.

He didn't yell. He didn't run.

He just walked toward them with a calm that terrified her more than any shouting ever had.

"Why are you making' this so hard?" he asked. "You think you grown? Think you smart? You aren't nothing' without me."

Alexis forced herself to meet his eyes.

"I'm not getting in your car."

A muscle in Rico's jaw twitched. "Girl, don't test me."

Then a voice cut through the street.

"She said no."

Devin.

He walked out from the alley, hands clenched, eyes cold.

Rico still had the advantage; older, meaner, more dangerous; but Devin didn't. back down.

"You going to hit me now, Rico?" Devin asked. "In front of the whole block? In front of your own kids?"

People were watching from windows, from stoops. The block loved a show. The block loved drama. But the block also loved gossip; and Rico hated being embarrassed.

He stared at Devin for a long moment.

Then he clicked his tongue, shook his head, and backed off.

"Keep running', Alexis," he said quietly. "You think you safe. But I always find what's mine."

He got back in the car, slammed the door, and drove off.

The second he turned the corner, Alexis's knees nearly buckled. Devin grabbed her arm. "You good?"

"No," she whispered. "But we will be."

She looked down at her siblings, their frightened eyes, their shaking hands.

She wasn't doing this just for herself.

She was doing it for them.

And the competition wasn't just a chance anymore.

It was the lifeline they needed.

That night, while the kids were huddling together for safety, Alexis finished her. architectural model with a level of focus she didn't know she had left.

She measured. She glued. She shaded. She refined.

When she finally placed the last piece at dawn, she stepped back and stared. Her building stood tall, strong, defiant; everything she wanted to become. Devin walked over, rubbing sleep from his eyes.

"Damn," he whispered. "Lex... it's perfect."

For the first time in her life, she let herself believe it. Tomorrow, she will enter that room.

Tomorrow, she will compete.

Tomorrow, she would prove that a girl from the block; a girl born into chaos and pain and nothing; could rise.

And when did she win?

She wouldn't be running anymore.

She would be rising.

Chapter Eight
The Room Where Futures Are Chosen

The morning of the competition felt unreal.

The city was still waking up; storefront gates sliding open, buses groaning down crowded streets, people rushing toward jobs they hated. But Alexis wasn't heading to survival today.

She was heading to possibility.

Devin walked beside her, carrying the protective box that held her architectural model. Her siblings trailed behind, dressed in their cleanest clothes; Jalen in a shirt a size too big, Mia with her hair in neat braids, Ty gripping a small toy car for courage.

They took two buses and walked four blocks until they reached the downtown Arts Center: tall glass windows, polished floors, everything too shiny for kids from their block.

Mia's eyes went wide. "Lex... are you sure we're allowed here?"

Alexis squeezed her hand. "We belong everywhere they tell us we don't."

Inside, the registration table buzzed with energy. Teen competitors carried large models, tubes of blueprints, and fancy art kits. Some arrived with parents in suits. Some had private tutors whispering last-minute advice in their ears.

Alexis stepped forward, conscious of the patchwork clothes on her siblings, the exhaustion under her eyes, the weight of everything she had fought to get here.

"Name?" the woman at the table asked. "Alexis Grant."

The woman scanned a list, handed her a badge, and nodded toward a row of tables. "You're in section C. Set up and wait for judging."

Alexis let out a slow breath. This was real.

This was happening.

Setting up wanted to step into another world.

She unpacked her model with precise hands, smoothing each edge, correcting minor smudges, making sure the structure stood perfectly. Her presentation board stood behind it; she had clean text, careful labels, sketches done with her best pencil strokes.

Competitors on either side watched her, some curious, some doubtful, some dismissive.

A boy with expensive sneakers and a portfolio thicker than a brick leaned over.

"Nice model," he said. "Did your mentor help you build it?" Alexis did not look up. "No."

"Your parents?" "No."

He smirked. "So... no guidance at all?"

Alexis finally met his eyes. "Yeah. And I am still here." The boy blinked and threw

26

it off. "Uh; okay
."
She went back to adjusting her baseboard.

The judges arrived half an hour later, three adults in tailored clothes, carrying clipboards and quiet authority. They moved slowly from table to table, studying each design, asking questions, whispering to one another.

As they got closer, Alexis felt her pulse go wild. Devin tapped her shoulder gently. "Breathe." Jalen whispered, "You're going to win, Lex."

Mia held her hand tight.

Ty stared at her with sleepy trust. And Alexis stood tall, ready.

"Alexis Grant?" the lead judge asked as they reached her display. "Yes," she said, hoping her voice did not shake.

They learned in, examining the structure, flipping through her blueprint packet, studying the presentation board.

"This is... ambitious," one judge murmured. "These support beams; this curvature here; this is complex work for someone your age."

Alexis nodded. "I wanted to design something that felt strong but welcoming. A space for families who need stability."

Another judge raised an eyebrow. "And what inspired that?"

A thousand memories flashed through her:

Her mother was crying. Her father yelling.

Her siblings trembling in stairwells. Nights on broken balconies.

Days spent dreaming of safety.

"A lack of it," she answered simply.

The judges paused, exchanging glances.

Then the lead judge asked, "What do you want, Alexis? Beyond this competition."

Alexis swallowed.

She could lie.

She could pretend she wanted prestige, success, or recognition.

But that wasn't her truth.

"I want to build something better than the life I came from," she said quietly. "For me. For my brother and sister. For anyone who has told they are stuck where they started."

The judges did not write anything for a moment.

They just looked at her.

Not at the girl from the block.

Not at the teenager with no parents behind her.

Not at the kid with secondhand clothes and a heavy past. But at the architect she was trying to become.

"Thank you, Alexis," the lead judge said softly. "We'll be announcing results shortly."

They moved on.

She finally exhaled.

Devin grinned. "You killed that."

Mia beamed. "You sounded like a grown-up!" Jalen nodded. "Like a boss."

But Ty tugged her sleeves and eyes wide. "Lex?" "What's wrong, honey?"

He pointed toward the entrance. A chill froze her blood.

Standing in the doorway, two security guards arguing with him for entry; Was her father.

Rico.

Face storm dark. Eyes locked on her. Moving closer. The room spun.

Devin stiffened. "Lex... go. Now."

Her siblings clung to her.

Rico shoved past security, shouting her name.

The judges turned. Competitors started. Parents whispered.

Everything she had built; every chance, every hope; was suddenly at risk.

Alexis grabbed her siblings' hands. "Run," she whispered.

Because the past did not like being left behind. And Rico wasn't ready to let her future go.

Chapter Nine
The Day Everything Cracked Open

Rico's voice cut through the room like a blade. "Alexis! Get over here!"

Heads turned. Whispers spread like wildfire. Judges paused mid-step. Competitors froze.

Alexis felt her legs tense, not from fear, but from years of learned survival. Devin stepped in front of her instinctively. "Rico, you need to leave. Now." Rico's eyes narrowed at him. "Move, boy. I'm not talking' to you."

The security guards caught up, grabbing Rico's arms, but he jerked them off with a violent twist.

Alexis pulled her siblings behind her. Her voice stayed low, steady. "Don't run. Stay right behind me."

Rico stalked toward them, chest heaving, jaw tight. His clothes were wrinkled, stained, his pupils too wide; he was high or crashing, and both were dangerous.

"You think you grown now?" Rico barked, pointing at her. "You walk out my house without a word? Take my kids? Embarrass me in front of my people?"

His voice boomed in the elegant hall, shaking the quiet.

"Rico;" Alexis started.

But he jabbed a finger at her face. "Don't 'Rico' me. You live under my roof, you. follow my rules. You aren't better than anybody. You aren't going' nowhere."

Alexis felt the same creep up; shame he'd taught her, shame she refused to carry. anymore.

Then she heard a small voice whisper behind her.

"Lex… I'm scared."

Ty.

And that fear snapped something inside her.

She stepped around Devin, facing her father fully.

"I'm not yours to control," she said, her voice ringing louder than she meant. "Not anymore. Not ever again."

Rico's face contorted with rage. He lunged.

Everything happened at once.

Security surged forward. Devin grabbed Alexis's shoulder, pulling her back. Mia screamed. Jalen backed up, shielding Ty.

Rico was inches from her when a firm hand wrapped around his wrist, twisting hard, stopping him from cold.

The room went silent.

Because the person gripping Rico wasn't security.

It was Ms. Ramirez; small, composed, and furious in a way Alexis had never seen. "You lay one hand on that child," she hissed, "and you'll answer to more than

30

security."

Rico tried to yank away, but Ms. Ramirez held on, surprising everyone, including Alexis.

Security piled in then, restraining him. Rico howled curses as they dragged him back toward the entrance.

"You aren't going to survive without me!" he shouted. "You hear me, girl? You aren't nothing without me!"

The doors slammed behind him. The silence was suffocating.

Alexis stood frozen, every muscle trembling, her heart in her throat, her siblings clinging to her.

The judges stared. Competitors whispered. Cameras might've been recordings she didn't know.

All she knew was she couldn't breathe.

Ms. Ramirez gently touched her shoulder. "Alexis... look at me."

She lifted her eyes.

"You are not defined by where you come from," Ms. Ramirez said slowly, clearly enough for everyone nearby to hear. "Today proved that."

Devin stood beside her. "You, okay?"

Alexis wanted to say yes. She wanted to pretend she was used to this, that drama and danger rolled off her.

But her voice cracked. "I... I didn't want them to see that."

"Them" meaning the judges.

Competitors.

The world she was trying to step into.

Ms. Ramirez shook her head. "What they saw was a young woman who stood her ground. Who protected her family." She glanced toward the judge panel. "They saw strength."

Alexis swallowed hard, unsure.

Because right now, she doesn't feel strong.

She felt exposed.

Small.

Like the girl from the broken apartment again.

After a long moment, one of the judges approached, an older woman with silver hair and warm eyes.

"Alexis," she said softly. "May I speak with you?"

Alexis nodded numbly, bracing for disappointment.

The judge lowered her voice. "We're aware that life is difficult for many of our students. What happened today does not count against you. In fact," She paused, choosing her words. "Your courage and composure were remarkable. Many adults couldn't have handled that."

Alexis felt her chest tighten. "So, I'm… not disqualified?" The judge smiled gently. "No, dear. The opposite."

Before Alexis could ask what that meant, the judge stepped back.

We'll be announcing results shortly," she said.

Alexis sank into a chair, her siblings gathering around her. Devin rested a steady hand on her back.

She stared at her shaking hands.

Rico was gone; for now.

But his words clung to her like a bruise.

You aren't anything without me.

She clenched her jaw. No.

She wouldn't let that voice echo in her head anymore. She wouldn't let him write her story.

This was her life. Her fight.

Her future.

She wiped her eyes, stood up straighter, and exhaled. Because no matter what happened next.

She had already survived something bigger than any competition.

Chapter Ten
The Announcement

The exhibition hall buzzed with tension, low whispers, shuffled feet, the restless tapping of nervous fingers. The judges stood on a raised platform near the front, clipboards tucked away, expressions unreadable.

Alexis stood with her siblings clustered around her, Devin beside her like a shield. Ms. Ramirez lingered a few feet away, giving her space but refusing to leave her alone. The chaos with Rico still hovered in the air, but now the room felt differently, watchful.

Contestants whispered, glancing at her way. Some looked sympathetic. Some curious. Others judgmental.

But no one ignored her anymore.

Alexis tugged at her presentation badge, hands steadier now but still warm with leftover adrenaline.

Jalen nudged her. "You think you won?"

She exhaled. "I don't know. Doesn't feel real." Ty tugged her leg. "I hope you get a big trophy." She smiled weakly. "Me too, baby."

The lead judge, Dr. Silverman, stepped forward and tapped the microphone.

"Thank you all for your patience," she began, voice echoing off the high ceilings. "This year's Youth Urban Design Competition has showcased extraordinary talent. Every one of you should be proud."

A murmur rippled through the crowd. Alexis held her breath.

Dr. Silverman continued. "We will begin by announcing third place."

Alexis collapsed her hands. Mia squeezed them tighter.

"Third place goes to… Jordan Wexler, for the 'Greenstone Community Garden Plan.'"

Applause broke out. Jordan; the boy with the expensive sneakers; flashed a grin and jogged up to the stage. His parents embraced him proudly.

Alexis swallowed the knot in her throat.

"Second place," Dr. Silverman said, "goes to… Melissa Carter, for her 'Riverside Youth Center Renovation.'"

Another wave of cheers.

Alexis could feel her pulse in her ears.

And then there was only one name left.

Dr. Silverman paused, scanning the crowd slowly, almost deliberately; before speaking again.

"And now… first place."

The room stilled. Not a whisper. Not a shuffle.

Alexis's stomach twisted.

34

"First place," Dr. Silverman said clearly, "goes to a young woman whose work stunned all of us."

Devin exhaled sharply. Mia started trembling.

Dr. Silverman continued, "Her design demonstrates technical strength, creativity, and emotional intelligence. She turned adversity into vision. She built not just a structure; but a story."

Alexis's heart thumped wildly.

"First place goes to… Alexis Grant."

The world froze. Then it roared.

Her siblings shrieked. Devin threw his arms around her. Ms. Ramirez covered her mouth, tears shining in her eyes.

Alexis stood still, stunned, barely believing her ears.

"Lex!" Mia squealed, shaking her. "You won!"

"Go!" Devin urged, laughing through disbelief. "Go get your trophy!"

Alexis moved as if underwater, her feet somehow carrying her toward the stage. People clapped. Some reached out to touch her arm as she passed. Others just stared. She didn't care.

She didn't see them.

She was seeing something else entirely; years of surviving, pushing, dreaming. She stepped onstage, blinked at the lights, and the judges smiled at her.

Dr. Silverman handed her a gold trophy, warm in her hands. "You earned this," she said softly. "Never doubt that."

Alexis's voice cracked. "Thank you."

The applause washed over her; loud, long, overwhelming.

For the first time in her life, people weren't seeing a problem. They weren't seeing a burden.

They weren't seeing the daughter of a drug addict or a pimp.

They were seeing her. And she felt weightless.

Back in the crowd, her siblings launched at her like excited puppies.

"You did it!" Jalen shouted. "You were so brave!" Mia cried.

Ty hugged her leg. "You're a hero, Lex."

Devin wrapped an arm around her shoulders. "I knew you had it in you. Always did."

For the first time in years, Alexis felt something blooming in her chest, something soft, warm, terrifying.

Hope.

But the celebration was interrupted when a stern voice called out from behind.

"Miss Grant?"

Alexis turned.

A woman in a navy blazer approached; polished, professional, important. Her badge identified her as Director of Youth Programs, City Housing & Development Initiative.

"Hi," Alexis said carefully.

The woman smiled. "I'd like a word, if you have a moment." Alexis straightened. "Yes, ma'am."

The director nodded. "Your project... it wasn't just impressive. It aligned perfectly with a new initiative we're launching. We're looking for youth ambassadors; interns, really; who can work with our teams on real community design work."

Alexis blinked. "Real... work?"

"Yes. You'd train with our architects, attend workshops, work on real blueprints. And the program comes with a stipend."

A stipend.

Real training.

A way out.

A way forward.

The director smiled warmly. "I think you'd be perfect for it."

Alexis felt her breath catch.

She had come hoping for a trophy. She was living with a future.

When the director walked away, Alexis stood still, stunned all over again.

Devin grinned, nudging her. "See? I told you. You're meant for bigger things."

Alexis stared at the trophy in her hands. For the first time ever.

She believed him.

Chapter Eleven
When Success Becomes a Target

The neighborhood looked different when Alexis stepped off the bus that evening; maybe because she was different now.

The trophy was tucked carefully in her bag, wrapped in her jacket so no one on the block would see it. Not because she was ashamed…

But because around here, shining too brightly could get you dimmed really fast. Her siblings ran ahead, laughing on the cracked sidewalk, Mia pretending the

Trophy was a magic wand, Jalen boasting they'd all be rich soon, Ty humming to himself.

Devin walked beside her, hands deep in his pockets. "How are you feeling?" Alexis shrugged, a smile tugging at her lips. "Like I'm floating."

"Good. You deserve a win."

But the closer they got to their building, the more grounded heavily she felt.

Their front steps were crowded with men drinking, smoking, arguing loud enough for the whole block to hear. A couple girls leaned against the railing, scrolling their phones, giving Alexis quick up-and-down looks.

She kept her chin up.

Mia whispered, "Don't let them look at you like that." Alexis squeezed her hand. "I'm not."

Inside, the hallway smelled like bleach trying and failing to kill mold. Ty covered his nose. Jalen kicked a loose tile. Devin guided them up the stairs.

Alexis knew Rico wasn't here; security had taken him God knows where. But that didn't erase the tension, the feeling of shadows creeping behind her.

She pushed open the apartment door.

Her mother was on the couch, wrapped in a blanket, eyes red and tired. The television glowed on mute. She looked up as her children filed in.

"Oh… hey, babies."

Mia walked over, hugging her. "Mom, guess what Lex;" "Mia," Alexis warned softly.

Her mother glanced at Alexis, noticing the nervous flicker in her eyes. "What happened? Y'all okay? You look like you been runnin'."

Devin chimed in before Alexis could speak. "Competition went good." "Good?" Jalen scoffed. "She won first place!"

Their mother blinked as if the words didn't register. "First place?" she echoed.

Alexis pulled the trophy from her jacket. The shiny gold caught the dim light of their living room.

Her mother stared.

Then a soft, trembling smile spread across her face; real, warm, painfully rare.

"Alexis… baby… you did that?"

Alexis nodded, throat tight.

Her mother reached out, touching the trophy like it was fragile glass. "You really… you really went and did something big."

Emotions swirled in Alexis; joy, relief, and a sadness she couldn't name.

"Yeah, Mama," she said quietly. "I did."

Her mother leaned back, wiping her eyes. "I been good at much… but you? You something' special. Don't let nobody take that from you."

Alexis froze.

Because for the first time in a long time, her mother sounded sober. Present. Clear.

And it nearly broke her.

After settling her siblings with dinner, Alexis stepped outside onto the fire escape. The evening breeze carried city noises, laughter, music, anger, and life all tangled together.

Devin climbed out beside her. "Lot happened today." "You can say that again."

"You scared about Rico?"

She didn't answer right away. She looked down at her hands; hands that used to tremble, hands that held onto fear for too long.

"I'm scared he won't stop," she admitted. "He showed up once. He'll show up again." Devin nodded. "Yeah… he might. But you're not alone this time."

Alexis leaned her head back against the railing. "Devin, I got that internship. They want me. Like… for real."

"I heard. Proud of you."

"I should be happy," she whispered. "But all I can think about is what could go wrong."

"Nothing's going to ruin this unless you let it."

She closed her eyes. "I can't just leave my siblings. Mom isn't stable. Rico… he's unpredictable."

"You aren't leaving them," Devin said softly. "You're leading them."

Alexis opened her eyes slowly.

Something in his voice stroked the fire inside her; not rage, not fear, but ambition. Hunger. Purpose.

"You going to take the internship, Lex?"

She looked out at the skyline, where skyscrapers blinked like promises.

"Yes," she said. "I'm taking it." Devin smiled. "Good."

"But…" she added, "I got to find a way to keep my family safe first." She didn't know how.

Not yet.

But Alexis had crossed a line today and stepped into a future she wasn't letting anyone drag her back from.

Not Rico. Not poverty. Not fear.

She was on her way somewhere bigger.

And she was taking her whole family with her.

Chapter Twelve
The System Knocks

The next morning began with a knock. Not a soft tap.

A firm, rhythmic knock that echoed through the thin apartment walls.

Alexis sat up instantly, heart thudding. Sunlight filtered through the blinds, striping the room in pale gold. Her siblings were still asleep; Ty curled against her, Mia sprawled sideways, Jalen drooling on his pillow.

The knock came again.

"Lex?" Devin whispered from the hallway. "You up?"

She eased Ty off her and stepped out. Devin stood by the front door, shirt wrinkled, eyes alert.

"You are expecting somebody?" he asked. "No."

Her mother stirred on the couch, rubbing her face. "Who at the door this early?"

Alexis moved to the peephole and froze.

Two people waited outside; a woman in a blazer holding a folder and a man with a badge clipped to his belt.

No…

Not today. Not after everything. She cracked the door open an inch.

"Ms. Grant?" the woman asked, voice professional. Alexis swallowed. "Yes?"

"I'm Ms. Whitaker with Child Services. This is Officer Jameson. We need to speak with you regarding an incident yesterday involving your father."

Alexis's stomach dropped.

She opened the door slowly. Devin stepped behind her, solid as a wall.

Ms. Whitaker offered a polite but practiced smile, the kind that said she dealt with broken homes every day. "We received a report from the Arts Center. Multiple witnesses described your father attempting to physically confront you."

Alexis clenched her fists. "He didn't touch me."

"That's good," Ms. Whitaker said gently. "But his behavior was concerning."

Officer Jameson flipped open a notepad. "We need to ask a few questions about your home environment. Your siblings. Your mother."

Alexis's pulse pounded. "My mother is trying. She;"

Her mother walked over, hair messy, blanket wrapped around her shoulders. "I'm their mom," she said, voice rough. "Whatever you need to ask, ask me."

Ms. Whitaker glanced at Alexis first, like she could sense the real stability in the room came from her.

"May we come in?" the caseworker asked.

Alexis hesitated.

Letting them in meant opening the door to everything, poverty, addiction, chaos. And once the system was in your business, it stayed there.

Devin touched her shoulder. "You don't have to do this alone." She exhaled shakily and stepped aside. "Come in."

The apartment suddenly felt smaller as the caseworker and officer inspected the space. Ms. Whitaker's pen moved constantly; notes about peeling paint, the half-working stove, the closet door that didn't close right.

Alexis hated every second.

She didn't want to be pitiful. She wanted progress.

Ms. Whitaker turned back to her. "Alexis, were you afraid of your father yesterday?"

Alexis hesitated. The lie was ready; No, he just showed up, that's all. A lie would make things easier today.

But not tomorrow.

"Yes," she admitted quietly. "I was."

Her mother sat heavily on the couch, eyes dimming with guilt. "He isn't supposed to come here no more. I told him that."

Officer Jameson nodded. "He was taken in last night. Disorderly conduct. He's being held for 48 hours."

Alexis let out a breath she didn't realize she was holding.

That gave her time. Space. A buffer.

Ms. Whitaker flipped her folder closed. "Given the incident, I'll be making a temporary safety plan. Not removal," she added quickly when she saw panic flash in Alexis's eyes. "But oversight."

"What kind of oversight?" Alexis asked.

"Regular check-ins. Support services for your mother. And we'd like to assign a youth advocate to you. Someone to help with the internship opportunity you were offered."

Devin's eyebrows lifted. "They already heard about that?"

Ms. Whitaker smiled. "The director called us. She wanted to ensure Alexis would be supported."

For the first time since they knocked, relief trickled in. Someone believed in her enough to protect her path. Alexis nodded. "Okay. I'll work with an advocate."

Ms. Whitaker stood. "Good. We'll be in touch. And Alexis?" "Yes?"

"You're doing an incredible job holding your family together." Her voice softened. "But you deserve people holding you up, too."

Alexis looked down, emotions rising unexpectedly. "Thank you."

With that, they left.

When the door closed, the apartment felt quiet. Heavy.

Her mother sank into the couch, covering her face. "I'm sorry," she whispered. "Rico keep messing' stuff up. I'm trying', Lex. I swear I am."

Alexis sat beside her. "I know, Mama. I know you're trying."

"But they are coming' in here now, watching' everything. What if they take y'all?"

"They won't," Alexis said, firm. "I'm not letting that happen."

Her mother looked at her; really looked; and for once didn't argue that she was. the parent.

Because sometimes survival made kids grow up first.

That afternoon, Alexis checked her email at the library computers.

SUBJECT: Welcome, Alexis – Internship Orientation

Her heart fluttered as she clicked it. Orientation was next week.

Her mentor assignment was attached.

There would be campus tours, blueprint labs, real architects.

She read the message twice, then three times, then printed the schedule like it was sacred.

Her life was changing. Fast.

Maybe faster than she could handle.

But she wasn't backing down.

Not now.

Chapter Thirteen
The First Door That Opened

Orientation day felt like stepping into another universe.

Alexis had borrowed one of Ms. Ramirez's blouse-lit blue, crisp, ironed; and paired it with her best jeans. Devin had braided her hair the night before, fingers gentle, careful, like he knew how important this day was. Her siblings shouted good luck from the fire escape as she boarded the bus, and for the first time, Alexis wasn't embarrassed.

She was excited.

The City Housing & Development building rose from the ground like a promise; sleek steel, wide windows, revolving doors that never stopped moving. People walked in and out with briefcases, lanyards, confidence.

Alexis swallowed hard. She belonged here.

She repeated that until her legs stopped shaking.

Inside the lobby, interns lined up for badges. Some wore pressed slacks and button-ups. Others clutched portfolios like armor. A few looked like they came from money. A few looked like they came from places like hers; back-of-the-bus kids, neighborhood kids, hungry kids.

A tall girl with box braids and thick-framed glasses stood behind Alexis, shifting. nervously. "You here for Urban Design?" "Yeah," Alexis said.

"I'm Jada," the girl offered. "Alexis."

"You excited?"

Alexis exhaled. "I'm terrified." Jada laughed. "Same."

Just like that, Alexis felt a little lighter.

After the badges were printed, the interns were led to a conference room with floor-to-ceiling windows overlooking the city. Alexis had never been this high up in a building before.

She pressed a hand to the glass, staring down at the tiny cars, the tiny people, the tiny worlds below.

One day, she thought, "I'm going to design something bigger than this.

A woman in a slate-gray suit stepped to the front of the room. Tall, composed, with sharp eyes that took in everything.

"Good morning. I'm Ms. Carter, Director of Youth Apprenticeships." Her voice filled the room. "And today, you begin the first step of your professional journey."

Alexis sat up straighter.

Ms. Carter continued, "Each of you will be paired with a mentor. These are architects, engineers, and planners who've volunteered to train you."

She lifted a clipboard. "When I call your name, you'll meet your mentor."

Alexis wiped her palms on her jeans. Her heart thudded with every name called.

"Jada Thompson," Ms. Carter announced.

Jada stood and was paired with a short woman with a tablet and a warm smile. They shook hands.

"Luis Martinez." "Emma Riley."

"Kevin Sun."

One by one, interns disappeared into clusters.

Alexis's pulse quickened.

Then.

"Alexis Grant."

She stood.

Ms. Carter gestured toward a man standing near the corner. Early 40s maybe, tall, brown-skinned, tailored shirt, sleeves rolled up, black glasses perched on his nose. He looked smart but approachable.

"This is Mr. Rowan Hale," Ms. Carter said. "Senior architect. He'll be your mentor."

Rowan stepped forward, extending his hand.

"Alexis," he said warmly. "Congratulations on winning the competition. I've been looking forward to meeting you."

She blinked. "You… have?"

"Yes. Your design showed a level of intuition most students don't develop for years." His voice was calm, steady. "I requested you."

Requested.

Requested her.

Something bloomed in her chest that was deeper than pride, validation.

She shook his hand, trying not to look as stunned as she felt. "Thank you. I; I'm ready to work."

"I'm sure you are," he said with a soft smile. "Let's get started."

He led her to a drafting workstation; her own desk, computer, drawing tools, grid pads, everything she had only ever seen in photos.

Her throat tightened.

"You'll use this space three days a week," Rowan explained. "I'll give you exercises, teach you software, expose you to real client work. You'll shadow me on site visits. It won't be easy."

"Good," Alexis said. "I don't want easy." He chuckled. "I like that."

As he walked her through the equipment, she noticed a few interns watching her. Whispering.

Side-eyeing.

She tried to ignore it; until one tall boy with soft curls and designer headphones around his neck openly smirked.

"You," he said to another intern, not bothering to lower his voice. "That's the girl from the Arts Center, right? The one whose dad crashed the event?"

Alexis's stomach was clenched.

Another boy snorted. "Yeah. Heard he got dragged out screaming."

They both laughed.

Rowan noticed the shift in her expression. "Everything alright?" Alexis forced a tiny nod. "Yeah. Fine."

But inside, anger twisted with shame.

No matter where she went, her past was right behind her; loud, messy, and uninvited.

Around lunch break, Rowan handed her a folder. "This is your first assignment. A Small ones just conceptual sketches. But I want you to think deeply."

Alexis flipped it open.

Design a rooftop community garden for a low-income building.

Her breath hitched.

"Why this?" she asked quietly.

Rowan leaned against her desk. "You understand communities others overlook. You see things people like me don't. I want to see that perspective in your work."

She nodded slowly. "I can do that." "I know."

At the end of the day, Alexis left the building with her assignment tucked safely in her backpack. Outside, she found Jada waiting near the bus stop.

"How'd it goes?" Jada asked.

Alexis smiled. "Better than I expected."

"As long as we survive the next week, we're good."

They laughed, and for a moment the world felt manageable.

But when Alexis reached her block, the familiar tension seeped back in.

A couple of Rico's boys lingered near the corner. They watched her too closely. One of them nodded at her. "You, Lex. Rico back tomorrow."

Her blood ran cold.

"We heard what happened." The guy smirked. "He isn't happy."

Alexis gripped her folder so tightly the edges bent.

Tomorrow.

He'll be out tomorrow.

Her trophy had opened a new door.

But her past was already waiting in the hallway.

Chapter Fourteen
The Return

Morning came too fast.

Alexis barely slept. Every time she shut her eyes, she saw Rico walking through the front door; lips curled, voice low, a storm waiting to drop. She'd seen him angry before. High before. Violent before.

But never humiliated.

And world traveled fast in their neighborhood. Too fast.

She pulled herself out of bed before the sun cracked the sky and checked on her siblings. All three were curled up together on the pullout mattress, the fan humming in the corner. They looked peaceful.

She needed to keep it that way.

By seven, she had breakfast started oatmeal stretched with water, brown sugar, and the smallest handful of raisins she'd saved from a snack pack Devin brought over earlier in the week. Not a feast, but enough.

She tried to focus on normal things: stirring, packing lunches, tying little shoes. But her stomach kept twisting, her ears tuned to every sound from the hallway.

At 7:43, she heard the elevator. At 7:44, footsteps.

At 7:45, the front door shook.

 Not knocked.

Shook.

"Open up, Lex," a voice growled. "I know you're in there."

Her heart slammed.

Before she could move, Devin stepped out of his room, pulling a T-shirt over his head. "Get the kids in the bathroom," he whispered. "Now." "What about;"

"Do it."

She ushered her siblings into the small bathroom, handed them her phone, and told them to watch cartoons and not open the door for anything. Then she locked it from the outside.

Just as she stepped back into the living room, the door flew open. Rico stood there. He looked smaller than she remembered, but also more dangerous; like a wild animal backed into a corner. His braids were undone, his clothes wrinkled, eyes bloodshot like he hadn't slept.

"You got some nerve," he slurred. Alexis didn't say a word.

"You think you can embarrass me? Make me look weak in front of everybody? You think your something' now?" Rico stepped inside, breathing sour fumes. "A Lil' trophy don't make you better than the streets that raised you."

Devin moved in front of Alexis before Rico got too close. "You need to leave, man." Rico ignored him. His eyes stayed locked on Alexis. "I'm talking' to her."

Devin repeated, voice firmer, "You need to leave."

Rico's attention shifted just long enough for Alexis to see the rage spark. "I'm not scared of you, boy."

Devin's fists clenched, but his voice stayed calm. "Doesn't matter. You still need to leave."

Rico smirked the kind of smirk that meant trouble. "What, you her bodyguard now? Her little boyfriend?"

Alexis spoke before Devin could react.

"We're done, Rico." Her voice was steady, even though her hands shook. "I don't need you. And you're not going to drag this family down with you anymore."

Rico's whole face twisted. "You think you can just walk away?" "I already did."

He took a step forward. Devin stepped forward too.

For one tense, breathless second, nobody moved. Then a voice boomed from the hallway:

"Everything okay in here?"

It was Ms. Thompson, their nosy; and blessed; neighbor. Behind her stood Mr. Albert and Mrs. Harris. Three elders. Three witnesses. Three people, Rico, didn't want to watch him.

Rico froze.

Ms. Thompson crossed her arms. "You are looking' for trouble, Rico?" Mr. Albert added, "Cause if so, we can call the police."

Rico backed up, jaw flexing, eyes darting. He knew he couldn't risk a parole violation.

on his first day out.

"This aren't over," he spat at Alexis.

Maybe not, she thought.

But today you don't win.

He stormed off, slamming the exit door at the end of the hallway so hard the walls shook.

Alexis let out a breath she didn't realize she'd been holding. Devin closed the door. and locked all three locks.

"You alright?" he asked.

She nodded, even though she wasn't sure.

After walking her siblings to school, she headed to her internship. Her hands were still trembling as she boarded the bus. Her mind replayed Rico's threats over and over like a broken loop.

By the time she reached the **Housing & Development** building, she had one goal:

Don't let anyone see you rattled.

Inside, Rowan was waiting at her desk.

"Morning, Alexis," he said. Then he paused, studying her. "You look… shaken. Everything alright?"

She wanted to lie. To say she was fine.

To say her morning didn't feel like surviving a war.

But her voice betrayed her.

"My father showed up."

Rowan's expression softened, not pity, but real concern. "Do you need to take the day off?"

"No." She sat down. "I need to be here."

"Okay." He nodded. "Then we'll work. But if you need a break, you take it. Understood?"

"Yes."

He slid a cup of hot cocoa toward her. "I thought you might like this." She blinked. "How did you;"

"You strike me as someone who forgets to take care of herself." She didn't trust her voice enough to reply.

Hours later, buried in sketches for the rooftop garden, she finally felt her heartbeat slow. Her lines became smoother, her vision clearer. She added benches, raised planters, shade canopies, and small playground features. She added color. Green. Yellow. Pink.

Life.

Somewhere safe.

Somewhere her siblings could breathe.

Rowan walked over, leaning slightly behind her. "That's beautiful." "It's not done." "But you are on the right path." She looked up at him. "Thank you." "For what?"

"For seeing me."

Rowan hesitated, then said quietly, "You deserve to be seen, Alexis."

That evening, when she stepped off the bus, she found her siblings playing tag on the sidewalk. Devin was watching them like a hawk. No Rico in sight.

"Everything's okay," Devin said gently, reading her fear.

She nodded, feeling the weight in her chest lighten just a little. For the first time all day, she allowed herself to breathe.

But later that night, as she lay in bed, staring at the cracked ceiling; She knew Rico would be back.

He always came back.

And next time, he wouldn't walk away so easily.

Chapter Fifteen
Plans in the Dark

The next few days were quiet. Too quiet.

Rico hadn't shown up. No calls. No messages. No random shadows lingering downstairs. But Alexis felt him everywhere; like smoke trapped in her clothes, like footsteps always half a block behind her.

Every time the elevator dinged, she tensed.

Every time a man with a hood passed by the corner shop, she checked twice. Devin noticed.

So did her siblings.

But nobody said a word.

Silence was safer than fear spoken out loud.

On Thursday evening, Rowan called the interns together for an announcement in the main workspace.

Everyone gathered around; clipboards, laptops, the hum of printers filling the room with the energy of something important.

Rowan stood in front of Ms. Carter, both of them looking unusually excited.

"We've been granted approval," Ms. Carter said, "for a new summer project. And we want one of our interns to help lead the conceptual development."

Whispers shot through the group. Lead?

A teenager?

"In two months," Rowan explained, "we will submit a proposal to convert a vacant lot in Easton Heights into a community hub; garden, playground, tutoring center, resource office, the works."

Alexis froze. Easton Heights. Her neighborhood. Her world.

Her siblings.

"This will be competitive," Ms. Carter continued. "We'll choose based on portfolio submissions due next week."

Jada nudged Alexis. "Girl. This is you." But Alexis wasn't sure.

She suddenly felt split in two; one half believing she could change her neighborhood, the other half remembering what it felt like to stand in her doorway with Rico threatening her.

Was she strong enough to hold both worlds?

After the meeting, Rowan caught up with her at her desk.

"Walk with me for a minute?"

They stepped into the hallway, lined with framed blueprints and architectural awards. The gentle hum of office chatter disappeared as the door eased shut behind them.

"I want you to apply," Rowan said, cutting straight to it. Alexis stared at the carpet. "I don't know if I'm ready." "You are."

She shook her head softly. "It's complicated." "Is it because of your father?"
She flinched.
He studied her, not praying; just waiting.
She finally whispered, "My neighborhood is dangerous. And everyone knows my business. If I step up like that... there'll be attention. Heat. Rico doesn't like attention."
Rowan's jaw tightened just enough to show anger; not at her, but at everything. she'd survived.
"You can't let him decide the size of your future," Rowan said gently. "People like him shrink the world around them. Don't let him shrink yours."
Her eyes were stung.
She looked away.
He continued, "You have vision, Alexis. Real vision. You understand what. communities need because you've lived it. That gives you a power most architects never develop."
She swallowed hard. "I'm scared."
"Being scared means you're close to something important."
No one had ever said that to her before. Her mother used fear as a weapon.
Rico used it as control. Teachers used it as judgment.
Rowan used it as a mirror.
"Let me help you," he said. "Let me mentor you through this submission. Step by step."
She finally nodded.
"Okay," she whispered. "I'll do it."
Rowan smiled. "Good. I'll be here every step of the way."
For once, she believed him.
That night, she sat at the kitchen table long after everyone fell asleep. Papers spread across the surfaces, sketches, notes, maps, and research she printed on the office printer when nobody was watching.
A notebook lay open in front of her with a title written in careful letters:
PROJECT EASTON RISING
She tapped her pencil against her lip, thinking through ideas. Safety.
 Green space.
After-school programs. Community pride.
Resources for families struggling like hers.
She sketched a multi-use space with murals on the walls, bright colors, solar-powered lights, benches shaped like leaves, and a tutoring center that stayed open

late so kids had somewhere to go beside the street.

She drew a garden with raised beds labeled for herbs, vegetables, fruit trees, and native plants.

She drew a play area fenced and safe, where kids like her siblings wouldn't have to dodge stray bullets during summer nights. She drew hope.

She didn't know she fell asleep at the table until a hand touched her shoulder.

Her eyes snapped open. Devin stood beside her, brows raised.

"You good?" he murmured. "Yeah. Just working."

He glanced at the drawings. "This for your internship?" "Yeah."

He nodded slowly, impressed. "This is… beautiful, Lex." "Thank you."

Devin pulled out the chair beside her. For a moment, he didn't say anything. Then: "You are thinking about leaving?"

Alexis stiffened. "What?"

He pointed at the pages. "You're planning something bigger than this place. Bigger than us. I can see it."

She didn't answer.

He leaned forward. "If you get the chance to go… go. Don't look back." She swallowed. "What about you guys?"

"I'll hold things down." His voice softened. "Just promise me you won't stay for us."

Her eyes burned. She blinked fast. "I'm not abandoning anyone." "You're saving us," he whispered. Her throat tightened.

Then, in the quiet of their dim kitchen, Alexis admitted something she had never said out loud:

"I'm scared if I leave… Rico might take it out on you or the kids."

Devin nodded slowly, like he'd already thought of that too. "We'll figure it out." "How?"

He hesitated. "I'm talking to someone. A youth counselor. They have relocation programs, emergency assistance, and safe households. I didn't want to tell you until I knew it was real."

Her eyes widened. "Devin… why didn't you"? "Cause you carry too much already." Her chest caved a little.

She didn't realize how much she needed to hear that.

At 2:17 a.m., after Devin went to bed, Alexis heard footsteps outside their door again. She froze.

But they kept walking.

And for the first time since Rico returned, she felt not powerless.

Chapter Sixteen
Boiling Point

The next week unfolded like a storm cloud waiting to break.

Alexis worked on the Easton Rising design every spare minute she had. Before school. After her internship. Late at night when the world was quiet enough to think without fear creeping into the room.

Her notebook filled with sketches and ideas; play spaces, rooftop gardens, small-business stalls, solar lighting, murals celebrating local heroes. Every line felt like a brick in a future she could almost touch.

But the neighborhood felt different. Tense.

Watchful.

Because Rico was back.

And the streets never forget a threat.

One afternoon, as Alexis walked home with her siblings, a girl around eighteen hurried toward her from the corner store. Skinny, jittery, hoodie too big for her frame. It was Keisha; one of Rico's old runners.

"Lex," Keisha whispered urgently. "He's looking' for you." Alexis froze. "Why?"

"He is mad now. Somebody told him you got yourself an internship, some fancy architect job." Keisha chewed her lips. "He thinks you think you better than him."

Alexis felt sick.

"I'm trying to get away. He won't let me go."

Keisha looked at the ground. "Isn't nobody gets away from Rico unless he says so." Alexis grabbed her siblings' hands tighter. "I'm not his property."

Keisha stepped back like she admired the bravery but didn't want any part of the fallout. "Just be careful, Lex. He's on that heavy stuff again. Makes him…

unpredictable."

The kind of unpredictable that got people hurt.

By the time Alexis reached her building, Devin was waiting on the front steps, jaw tight.

"I heard," he said. "Keisha?"

He nodded. "We got to move fast."

"What does that even mean?" Her voice cracked from pressure. "We can't just disappear overnight."

Devin rubbed his face. "I talked to the youth counselor again. There's an emergency relocation program. But we'd have to report Rico officially."

Alexis stiffened. "You know what happens if we do that." "He goes back to jail."

"And then his boys come for us." Devin didn't answer.

He didn't need to.

They both knew the truth:

There were no safe choices. Only dangerous ones.

The next day at her internship, Alexis couldn't concentrate. She stared at her computer screen as lines blurred. Her heart thudded so fast she couldn't hear her. own thoughts. Rowan noticed. He always noticed.

"Walk with me," he said gently.

They stepped into a quiet conference room with tall windows and soft lighting. Rowan closed the door behind them.

"What's going on?"

Alexis hesitated; then the whole story poured out. Rico. The threats. The neighborhood tightening around her. Devin's relocation plan. Her fear of running. Her fear of staying.

By the time she finished, her hands were shaking.

Rowan sat across from her face unreadable but eyes burning with something fierce; anger, compassion, maybe both.

"You're in a dangerous situation," he said carefully. "And you need support. Real support. Not kids your age. Not from neighbors. From adults who can intervene."

She bristled. "We don't trust the system. It's never helped us." "And has staying silent ever protected you?"

She looked away.

Rowan leaned forward. "I'm not telling you to report him. That's your decision. But you don't have to handle this alone." His voice softened. "Let me connect you with someone who knows how to navigate situations like this. Safely."

Her throat tightened. "Why are you helping me so much?"

Rowan's voice was quiet but firm. "Because you matter. And because your talent deserves a chance to survive."

No one had ever said words like that to her. Not without wanting something back. She blinked fast, fighting tears.

"Okay," she whispered. "I'll talk to someone." "I'll arrange it today."

That evening, things came to a head.

Alexis and Devin met Ms. Carter after hours in her office. Rowan sat in the corner, giving them space but not leaving them alone.

Ms. Carter listened closely as Alexis explained everything, her father, the threats, the fear of retaliation.

When she finished, Ms. Carter didn't look shocked.

She looked angry.

"You deserve safety," she said firmly. "And your siblings do too." "I don't want them in foster care," Alexis said quickly.

"They won't be," Ms. Carter assured her. "Our office partners with community advocates who specialize in family relocation. Devin is old enough to serve as guardian. And if you relocate through an official program, Rico won't know where you go."

Alexis breathed shallow, heart hammering.

"This won't be easy," Ms. Carter added. "But it can work." Devin nodded. "What do we need to do?"

Ms. Carter opened a folder. "We file a confidential protection request. Then we move you to emergency housing until a permanent relocation is ready."

Alexis swallowed. "How soon?"

Ms. Carter met her eyes.

"Tonight."

Alexis's heart stopped. "Tonight?" she repeated.

"Yes. Rico's behavior is escalating. We can't take risks."

Everything went still. The office.

The air.

Her thoughts. Tonight.

She looked at Devin.

He nodded once. "We're ready."

She looked at Rowan.

He gave a small, steady nod.

Then she looked at her own trembling hands.

And she realized; Maybe she was ready too.

They packed in twenty minutes.

One backpack per person, Ms. Carter said.

Alexis grabbed essentials: schoolwork, sketches, one change of clothes for each sibling. Her siblings were confused, scared, but she kept her voice steady. Devin worked fast, efficiently, focused on keeping the little one calm.

They met Ms. Carter and a relocation officer behind the building. The officer drove a plain white Vanunu label, with no markings.

"Where are we going?" her youngest brother whispered. "Somewhere safe," Alexis said softly.

He nodded, trusting her completely.

Trust, she couldn't break.

As they climbed into the van, Alexis looked up at the building; her home, her history, the place she survived.

The place she almost stayed trapped. Behind the dumpsters, a shadow shifted. Rico.

He was watching.

His face twisting with fury and disbelief. He stepped forward.

But the relocation officer slammed the door shut and the van pulled away fast, tires screeching.

Alexis watched Rico grow smaller in the rear window, his figure swallowed by darkness.

Her hands shook. Her breath hitched.

But she didn't look away.

Not until the building disappeared behind them. Not until the fear inside her cracked open; And something new rushed in.

Freedom.

Terrifying. Uncertain. Real.

Chapter Seventeen
A Different Kind of Silence

The emergency housing unit was nothing like home. And maybe that was the point. The relocation officer guided them through a security door into a brightly lit hallway painted soft blue. Cameras lined the ceiling. Every door had an electronic lock. It smelled faintly like a lemon cleaner and laundry soap clean, sterile stillness Alexis wasn't used to.

"This is temporary," the officer explained. "A few days, maybe a week. Till placement is ready."

Temporary.

Everything in her life felt temporary.

He opened the door to a small suite: two bunk beds, a pullout couch, a kitchenette, a bathroom with soap packets still wrapped in plastic. Nothing warm. Nothing familiar.

But it was safe.

Devin scanned the room, impressed despite himself. Her siblings ran from bed to bed, poking at the stiff pillows and testing the light switches like they'd entered a secret hideaway.

Alexis stood in the doorway, backpack slung over one shoulder, staring.

No yelling.

No broken locks.

No footsteps outside the door waiting to pounce.

Just… silence.

It hit her harder than she expected.

The officer handed Devin a packet. "These are instructions. Meal hours. Security numbers. Evening check-in protocol. You're the guardian for the kids while you stay here."

Devin nodded confidently, though his hand trembled slightly on the folder.

"And you," the officer turned to Alexis, "will have someone assigned to check on. your emotional safety as well. Trauma counselors are available on-site." Alexis's brows lifted. "I don't need;"

The officer raised his hand gently. "Everyone says that. But you've been through a lot."

Devin shot her a look.

The kind that said: Maybe just let them help.

She nodded reluctantly.

After the officer left, Devin closed the door and locked it. Each click of the bolt felt like a weightlifting off her chest.

"We're safe," he whispered.

Alexis sank onto the bottom bunk, letting her backpack thud to the floor. "I don't know if it feels real yet."

"It will."

She wanted to believe him.

They put the younger kids to bed first. Her little sister refused to sleep unless she was holding Alexis's shirt, so Alexis lay on the bottom bunk beside her until her breaths deepened.

Once they were finally asleep, Devin pulled two metal chairs to the kitchenette table. "Come sit. We need to plan."

She joined him, the overhead light flickering slightly.

"We're going to be here until they find a long-term spot," he said. "They said maybe a new neighborhood. Maybe another borough."

Alexis's tense. "Another borough?"

"Safer schools. More resources. More distance."

She pressed her palms together. "What about my internship? My project?" "You'll stay in the city. Rowan said he would help with transportation." Her chest warmed. She hadn't realized he'd already followed up.

She nodded. "And school?" "They'll arrange it. But Lex..." He hesitated.

She looked up. "What?"

"When we move... you might have to cut ties with a lot of people. For good."

She swallowed.

Jada.

Ms. Ramirez.

The neighbors who stepped in.

The streets she knew like the lines on her palms. And Her mother.

The thought came sharp, painful, unexpected.

Her mother wasn't part of their household anymore, lost in her addiction and whatever man kept her couch to couch, but still... losing her completely felt like losing a limb she no longer used but still felt.

Alexis whispered, "What if she looks for us?"

Devin shook his head softly. "She hasn't looked for us in years."

Alexis blinked hard, but the truth stung anyway.

He reached across the table and squeezed her hand. "We're building something new. But that means letting go of the old."

Her voice cracked. "I don't know if I'm ready."

"You don't have to be ready," Devin said. "You just have to move."

65

Later that night, after Devin fell asleep on the pullout couch, Alexis quietly pulled out her sketch notebook. The lamp near the bunk cast a warm circle of light on the page.

She flipped to the Easton Rising project.

Her lines were confident now. Determined. But the vision felt different tonight. Less about buildings.

More about people.

More about survival.

More about rebirth.

She added lights along pathways; motion sensors, energy-efficient, reliable. She added a small resource office near the playground, with a sign that read: You're Not Alone.

She added security cameras. Not to trap people.

To free them.

When she finished, she exhaled shakily.

She wanted to cry but couldn't.

The tears were there; just stuck somewhere deep, waiting for permission to fall. A soft knock tapped the open doorway of the bunk area.

She looked up.

A woman stood there, mid-forties, soft brown skin, short curls, a kind face behind glasses. She wore a polo shirt with the emergency housing logo.

"Alexis Grant?" the woman asked gently. Alexis stood. "Yes?"

"I'm Nina. Night-shift trauma counselor." Her smile was warm, not pitying. "I was told not to disturb you unless you were awake. I saw your light."

Alexis stiffened immediately. "I'm fine."

Nina nodded like she'd expected that answer. "Can I sit?" Alexis hesitated... then nodded.

Nina sat on the bunk across from her, folding her hands in her lap.

"You don't have to talk," Nina said. "Just know that the shaking in your hands. The way you keep checking the door. The way you haven't cried yet. Those are all normal trauma responses."

Alexis's throat tightened. "I'm not traumatized."

Nina smiled softly. "You're brave. That's not the same thing."

Something inside Alexis cracked. Just a hairline fracture.

But enough.

Nina continued, voice gentle but steady: "You've been protecting your siblings, your brother, yourself. You've been building a life while surviving violence. Now your

66

brain doesn't know what to do with the quiet."

Alexis felt the tears finally gather. Burning.

Stubborn.

"Is that… bad?" she whispered.

"It means you're in the first stage of healing." A tear rolled down Alexis's cheek.

It was her first day.

Nina handed her a tissue. "You're safe now, Alexis. Safe enough to fall apart a little."

Alexis wiped her cheek, breath hitching.

"I don't know how to fall apart."

"That's okay," Nina said softly. "I'll teach you."

And for the first time in her life.

Alexis let herself cry.

Not silently. Not hidden. Not punished.

Just cried.

And when she was done, she felt lighter. Still scared.

Still uncertain.

Still grieving everything she'd lost.

But lighter.

She fell asleep that night curled around her sketchbook, the remnants of tears drying on her face, the weight of the world finally slowly lifting.

Tomorrow will be her hardest day yet. But tonight?

Tonight, she rested.

Chapter Eighteen
Blueprints of a New Life

The next morning, Alexis woke before the sun. Not from fear.

Not from yelling. Not from chaos.

But from habit; her body still tuned to survival, even in a place built for safety. She lay still for a moment, listening.

The soft snoring of her little brother. The hum of the mini fridge.

The distant sound of a security guard doing rounds in the hallway.

No shouting. No threats. No Rico.

She sat up slowly, rubbing sleep from her eyes.

Her sketchbook was still tucked under her pillow, pencil marks smudged on her wrist. For the first time in days, her mind felt clear enough to think about something besides survival.

The submission was due in two days.

She had no scanner here.

No way to print her renderings.

No quiet workspace except the bunk bed she shared with her sister.

But she wasn't giving up.

She had come too far.

After breakfast in the communal dining room, Alexis and her siblings met Devin in the courtyard. The emergency housing complex wasn't fancy; just a converted dorm building; but it had trees, a playground, and a garden in the back where volunteers tended tomatoes and herbs.

It was the safest place they had lived in years.

"Ms. Carter called," Devin said, pulling Alexis aside while the kids ran to the swings. "She arranged transportation back to your internship today."

Alexis blinked. "Already?" "She said Rowan insisted."

Her heart made a weird flip she didn't want to analyze.

Devin added, "I'm going with you. At least the first day."

Alexis nodded, relieved.

She didn't want to admit it, but the idea of returning to the city; even the good parts; felt overwhelming.

A black SUV with tinted windows arrived mid-morning. A relocation officer sat in the front seat, nodding professionally.

"Miss Grant? Ready?"

Alexis swallowed.

Ready?

No.

But going anyway.

She hugged her siblings, held her sister longer than necessary, then followed Devin to the car. As it pulled away from the safehouse, she watched the building shrink in the rear window just like she'd watched her old apartment shrink the night before.

Except this time, she wasn't leaving danger.

She was leaving safely to step back into her future.

At the Housing & Development building, Rowan met her in the lobby.

He looked relieved the moment he saw her; shoulders loosening, eyes softening behind his glasses.

She wasn't used to people looking relieved to see her. "Morning" he said gently. "How are you holding up?" She shrugged. "Trying."

"That's enough."

He walked with her to the elevator, giving Devin a respectful nod. Devin gave one back, but his eyes lingered on Rowan a little too long protective, assessing.

Rowan seemed to pick up on it but didn't comment.

When they reached the intern workroom, Jada practically tackled Alexis with a hug. "Girl, where have you been? Rumor, was you got sick or something." Alexis forced a thin smile. "Something like that."

Jada didn't push. That's why Alexis liked her.

Rowan handed Alexis a sleek tablet and a stylus. "I figured this might help with your design work."

She stared. "Is this... permanent?"

"It's assigned to you for the project." He smiled. "You earned it."

Her chest warmed.

Inside the folder of digital files, Rowan had already scanned the sketches she'd brought two weeks ago.

"You scanned these?" she asked softly.

"You left them open on your desk last week. I thought you might need them later."

She didn't know what to say.

No one had ever supported her work like this.

Not at school.

Not at home.

Not in the neighborhood. Only Rowan.

Her voice cracked. "Thank you."

He nodded once. "Let's get to work."

For the next two hours, Alexis poured herself into the digital version of her design. The stylus glided across the screen as she added shading, angles, light sources.

Rowan stayed nearby; not hovering, not controlling; just present.

"Try a softer curve on this edge," he suggested. "Make the raised beds ADA accessible."

"Show me what it looks like with night lighting."

She followed every note, adjusting, refining, improving.

By noon, she had something that actually looked professional. Something she could be proud of.

Something that felt worthy of all she'd fought through.

During lunch break, Ms. Carter stepped into the workroom with an envelope in her hand.

"Alexis? Can I speak with you for a moment?"

Alexis's stomach twisted. Had something gone wrong? Did Rico find them? Was the safehouse pulling them out?

She followed Ms. Carter into the hallway, Devin trailing close behind.

Ms. Carter held out the envelope. "This arrived this morning. We forwarded it through your relocation caseworker so it wouldn't reach your old address."

Alexis's pulse hammered. "Who's it from?"

Ms. Carter hesitated. "It's from your mother." Alexis's breath caught. Her mother.

The woman who disappeared into addiction.

The woman who left them to fend for themselves.

The woman Alexis both loved and resented in equal measure.

Her hands shook as she took the envelope. It was thin. Light. Rushed handwriting scrawled her name.

She stared at it, frozen.

"Do you want time alone?" Ms. Carter asked.

Devin stepped closer. "Lex... I can stay if you want."

She shook her head.

Then nodded.

Then she shook her head again.

Her voice came out small, unsure. "I... I don't know."

Ms. Carter touched her shoulder gently. "There's no right answer. But whatever's there, it doesn't have to define your next steps."

Alexis swallowed.

Then she slit open the envelope.

Inside was a single piece of lined notebook paper. Her mother's handwriting, shaky and uneven: Lex, I heard you won something. Some contest. People say you're going places. I don't get much but I'm proud of you.

I know I been a good mom. I know I left you with too much. But you have always
been strong. Stronger than me.
If you move away, I hope it's somewhere safe. Don't come looking for me. Just keep
going. Love you, Ma.
Alexis stared at the letter. Her throat burned.
Her vision blurred.
Her mother wasn't apologizing for everything. She wasn't promising change.
She wasn't asking for forgiveness.
She was letting her go.
Alexis folded the letter carefully, hands trembling. Devin placed a hand on her back.
"You, okay?"
She nodded slowly.
"Yes," she whispered. "I think… I think I am."
In a strange, aching way, the letter felt like closure. Not perfect.
Not clean.
But real.
And for the first time, Alexis felt something shift inside her. A door closing.
 Another door opening.
When she returned to the workroom, Rowan saw immediately that she'd been.
crying.
He didn't ask why.
He simply said, "Whenever you're ready… we can keep building the future you
deserve."
And Alexis sat down, wiped her eyes, and picked up the stylus. Because she was
ready.
Not to forget. Not to run.
But to rise.

Chapter Nineteen
Presentation Day

Two days later, Alexis stood in front of the mirror in the community center's donated clothing room, smoothing the front of her button-down blouse. It was slightly too big, sleeves rolled once, but it looked professional. Adult. Like someone who belonged in boardrooms and project meetings, not emergency shelters.

Devin waited outside the door with her siblings, all of them dressed in the cleanest clothes they owned. They were coming with her to the presentation. Ms. Carter insisted it would be a good learning experience. Devin insisted he wasn't letting her go alone.

Alexis took a steady breath. Today was the day.

Her chance to prove she wasn't just the girl from the projects. Not just a runaway. Not just someone surviving chaos. She was a designer.

A creator.

A girl with a mind that deserved space in the room.

She grabbed her tablet, held her chin up, and stepped out.

"You got this," Devin said.

Her sister Mia hugged her leg. "You look like a grown-up." Alexis laughed. "Don't rush it."

The Housing & Development building's main conference room looked even bigger than she remembered. A long table took up the center, surrounded by chairs filled with board members, architects, city planners, and the director of Youth Initiatives. Jada waved wildly from the back row, mouthing You better kill this.

Rowan stood near the projector, checking cables. When Alexis walked in, he gave her that soft, grounding smile.

"You ready?" "As I'll ever be."

"Good. Because they're excited to hear from you."

Excited.

To hear from her.

The idea still didn't feel real.

He handed her a small remote to click through slides. "Just talk about your vision. Everything else will follow."

She nodded, exhaling slowly.

When the director called her name, Alexis stepped to the front of the room.

Her heartbeat thudded loudly in her ears. Her palms were damp.

But when the lights dimmed and her first slide appeared on the screen glowing digital version of the garden courtyard she'd designed; something inside her settled.

This was her work. Her story.

Her voice. She began.

"At first glance, this might look like an ordinary community space. But where I grew up, places like this didn't exist. We had cracks in the concrete, broken swings, and abandoned buildings. So, when I designed this courtyard, I wanted it to feel the opposite of that. I wanted it to feel like hope."

She clicked the remote.

Next slide: benches with built-in charging ports, raised garden beds, safe walkways, soft lighting.

"I added solar lighting so kids can come here even in the evenings. And the garden beds are wheelchair accessible. I wanted everyone to have something here; parents, elders, teenagers, little kids."

Another clicks.

A blueprint layout appeared.

"I used every inch of available space to make sure nothing goes to waste. Because where I'm from, we learn to create something out of nothing."

She spoke steadily, confidently, her voice rising with each sentence.

And when she reached the final slide; an animation of the courtyard glowing at dusk; the room was silent. Not from boredom.

From impact.

She could feel it.

She could breathe it.

When she finished, there was a full second of stillness... then the room erupted into applause.

Real applause. Not pity.

Not politeness.

Respect.

Alexis felt warmth rush to her face, her chest tight with pride she had never allowed herself to fully feel.

Rowan met her eyes from the side of the room; expression filled with something like awe.

After the presentations, the judges held a short deliberation. The interns gathered in the hallway, pacing and whispering. Jada kept squeezing Alexis's arm. "Girl, if you don't win this, the whole system is rigged."

Alexis laughed nervously. "I just want a chance." Then the director stepped out, holding a folder. Everyone fell silent.

"We were incredibly impressed with all four finalists," he said. "But one design stood out; not just in creativity, but in purpose, clarity, and heart."

Alexis felt her stomach twist.

"The winner of this year's Urban Youth Initiative Grant is... Alexis Grant." For a moment, she didn't move.

Didn't breathe.

Jada screamed.

Devin let out a loud "YES!" from behind her.

Her siblings tackled her legs, cheering. But Alexis just stood there, stunned.

She'd won.

She'd actually won.

The director shook her hand. "Your design will be built as the prototype community space in the Lakeside Redevelopment Project. And you'll receive a $5,000 scholarship for continuing studies in architecture."

Five. Thousand. Dollars!

Her knees almost buckled.

Rowan stepped up next, pride written all over him. "You earned this, Alexis." She swallowed, eyes stinging. "Thank you for believing in me."

"I didn't believe in you," he said softly. "I saw you. You believed in yourself."

Her throat tightened.

But the moment that truly broke her up came when she turned and saw her brother, the usually quiet one, wiping his eyes.

"You made it, Lex," he whispered. "You really made it." She knelt, pulling all three of her siblings into her arms. "No," she said, voice shaking. "We did."

As the crowd buzzed, reporters took photos, and staff members congratulated her, Alexis stepped aside for a moment, breathing in the reality around her.

She was no longer just a girl fighting to escape. She was a girl who built something new.

For herself.

For her family.

For the community that made her tough enough to climb out. And for the first time in her life, she could see her future clearly. Blueprints and skies.

Concrete and dreams.

She didn't just rise.

She soared.

Chapter Twenty
Shadows That Don't Stay Gone

The week after Alexis won the grant, he felt unreal; like she was floating just above her own life.

Every morning, she woke up in the safehouse to see the sunlight instead of shouting.

Every afternoon, she walked into the **_Housing & Development_** building where adults nodded at her like she belonged.

Every evening, she worked with Rowan on refining the final specs for the prototype build.

It was everything she had dreamed of. Almost.

Because even in the quietest moments, Alexis felt the shadow of her past trailing her like a second heartbeat. Rico was out there somewhere. And people like him didn't just disappear.

She didn't tell Devin her fear. She didn't tell her siblings.

She didn't even tell Ms. Carter.

But Rowan noticed.

He always noticed.

One afternoon, after hours of drafting and note-taking, Rowan leaned back in his chair. "You're distracted," he said gently. Alexis blinked. "I'm fine."

He raised an eyebrow. "You don't have to be."

She hesitated before answering. "Winning this changes everything for my family. But Rico... he doesn't just let go."

Rowan nodded slowly. "Then we stay ahead of him." "We?"

"You're not alone in this, Alexis."

Something warm and unsettling moved in her chest. But before she could respond, Ms. Carter knocked on the glass wall.

Her face was tight. Serious.

"Alexis," she said carefully, "I need a word with you. Now."

In the hallway, Devin stood waiting; jaw clenched, fists bawling, stormy eyes. Alexis felt her stomach twist.

"What happened?" she asked.

Ms. Carter exchanged a look with Devin.

"We received a report from the relocation officer," she said. "Someone tried to approach the safehouse earlier today."

Alexis's pulse spiked. "Who?"

"We can't confirm yet. Security intervened before he reached the entrance." Devin stepped forward. "Lex... they said he was asking for you."

Her throat closed.

Rico.

It had to be Rico.

"Are my siblings okay?" she asked, voice trembling.

"They're safe," Ms. Carter assured. "The staff followed protocol immediately."

Alexis steadied herself against the wall. "What do we do now?"

"We increase security," Ms. Carter replied. "And we prepare for the possibility that he may keep trying."

For a moment, the hallway felt too small. Too airless. Too much like her old life choking its way back in.

But she wouldn't let it.

Not this time.

That evening, back at the safehouse, Alexis sat with her siblings during dinner. They laughed, argued, passed cornbread, talked about school like nothing was wrong.

She watched them; really watched them.

Mia with her missing front tooth, giggling about a boy who gave her a gel pen. Jace showed off his spelling test like it was a trophy.

Andre teasing everyone but eating more than all of them combined. They deserved this peace.

She'd fight for it.

After bedtime, Devin found her sitting on the edge of her bunk, staring at her.

mother's folded letter. "You, okay?" he asked.

"I'm tired of running," she said quietly.

"You're not running anymore," Devin assured. "You're rebuilding." She met his eyes. "Then why does it still feel like my past owns me?"

He sat beside her, lowering his voice. "Because it takes time. And because Rico… he's a storm. You're just now learning what sunlight feels like."

She exhaled shakily. "I hate that he still has any power over my life."

"But he doesn't," Devin said. "Not really. He's chasing a version of you that doesn't exist anymore."

Alexis swallowed hard. "I want him gone, Devin. For good." "Then we'll face him. Legally. Safely. Smart."

She nodded slowly. "I'll talk to Ms. Carter tomorrow." His smile was small but proud. "That's the Lex I know."

Later that night, long after Devin left, Alexis opened her sketchbook. She didn't draw buildings this time. She drew four figures. Small.

Huddled.

But standing together.

Behind them, she drew a tall shape; a looming silhouette of a man she didn't name.

Then she drew a wall rising between the group and the shadow. Strong. Solid. Unbreakable.

Not running. Not hiding.

Protecting.

She stared at the page, whispering to herself:

"I'm not afraid of you anymore."

For the first time, she meant it.

But the next morning, while she was getting ready for her internship, there was a knock on the safehouse director's office door.

A security officer handed over a small, sealed evidence bag. Inside was a folded piece of paper.

With Alexis's name written on the front. And the handwriting was unmistakable. It wasn't her mother's this time.

It was Rico's.

Alexis felt every hair on her arms rise. She had stepped into her future.

But her past had just stepped in after her.

Chapter Twenty-One
Pressure Points

The note didn't leave Alexis's hands all night.

Rico's handwriting; slanted, confident, familiar in the worst way; felt heavier than the paper it was written on. She read it again while the safehouse slept, the words pressing into her chest like a warning she couldn't ignore.

You took what's mine.

That wasn't anger.

That was ownership.

And Rico had never let go of anything he believed belonged to him.

The Warning Signs

By morning, Ms. Carter had already escalated security. Two additional guards. Restricted movement. No unscheduled outings.

Alexis stood at the kitchen sink, staring out at the quiet street beyond the fence.

"He's not bluffing," she said softly.

Ms. Carter joined her. "No. He's testing you." "Testing what?"

"How much pressure it takes to make you bend." Alexis clenched her jaw. "I won't."

Ms. Carter studied her carefully. "I believe you. But people like Rico don't stop because they're told to. They stop when they're cornered."

Alexis turned. "Then we corner him."

Cracks in the Past

Later that afternoon, Devin sat across from Alexis in the common room, his voice low.

"I checked with some people from the old block," he said. "Rico's been moving strange. Selling things. Laying low."

"Running?" Alexis asked.

"Preparing," Devin corrected. "Which usually means he's planning something ugly."

Alexis's stomach tightened. "My siblings?"

"Safe," Devin assured. "But Rico's been asking questions. About you. About Andre especially."

That name landed like a punch.

"Why Andre?"

Devin hesitated. "I don't know. But when men like Rico start narrowing in on one kid... it's never for nothing."

Alexis's pulse spiked.

Andre had been quieter lately. Watching more. Saying less. Seeing more than he ever should have.

The Unspoken Fear

That evening, Alexis sat beside Andre as he colored at the table.

"You okay, Dre?" she asked gently. He nodded too fast. "Yeah."

She watched him carefully. "You know you can tell me anything, right?" Andre's crayon paused.

"Even stuff about Rico?"

His shoulders tense.

Alexis's heart sank.

Andre whispered, "He told me not to talk about things I saw." Alexis's blood went cold. "What things?"

Andre shook his head quickly. "I don't want to get you in trouble."

Alexis pulled him into her arms, holding him tightly. "You could never get me in trouble. Ever."

Andre didn't say anything else; but his silence said enough. Alexis felt the pieces shifting into place.

Rico wasn't chasing memories.

He was chasing secrets.

A New Level

That night, Ms. Carter convened another meeting, security, legal advisors, and a Uniformed officer Alexis hadn't seen before.

"This is Officer Hale," Ms. Carter said. "He's with a special unit."

Officer Hale nodded. "We believe Rico's involvement goes beyond what we initially suspected."

Alexis sat straighter. "How far beyond?"

"Far enough that his interest in your family isn't personal; it's strategic."

Devin cursed under his breath.

Officer Hale continued, "If he believes someone in your household witnessed or overheard something damaging, he'll try to retrieve or silence them."

Alexis's chest tightened. "Andre." Hale didn't deny it.

Ms. Carter placed a steady hand on Alexis's arm. "That's why we're recommending Level Three relocation. Tonight."

Alexis exhaled shakily. "Do it."

Crossing the Line

As the sun set, the safehouse buzzed with controlled urgency. Packing. Paperwork. Quiet voices.

Alexis knelt in front of her siblings. "We're moving again. Just for safety."

Mia groaned.

Jace asked questions.

Andre stayed silent; but his eyes stayed locked on Alexis.

"You trust me?" she asked him softly. Andre nodded. "Always."

That promise was wrapped tight around her heart.

The Final Straw

Just before they boarded the transport, Alexis's phone buzzed.

A blocked number. One text.

"You should've stayed gone."

Alexis stared at the screen, something inside her snapping clean in two. Fear drained away.

What replaced it was sharp. Focused. Unmovable.

She handed the phone to Ms. Carter. "He crossed the line." Ms. Carter nodded grimly. "Yes. And now… so do we."

As the vehicle doors closed and the city lights blurred past, Alexis looked straight ahead.

Rico thought pressure would break her. But pressure had forged her.

And whatever secret Andre carried; Whatever truth Rico was running from; Alexis would protect it.

At any cost.

Chapter Twenty-Two
The Line That Can't Be Crossed

The safehouse meeting room was too quiet.

Alexis sat at the long table, hands clasped, knuckles pale. The security officer stood near the door, arms crossed. Ms. Carter reviewed a stack of printed notes. Devin paced in the corner like a caged lion.

And lying in the center of the table, protected by a plastic evidence bag, was a second note from Rico.

The one Alexis had found taped to the inside gate of the safehouse that morning.

Ms. Carter finally exhaled and pushed the paper forward. "We verified the handwriting. It matches the first message."

Alexis didn't flinch. She already knew.

Devin stopped pacing. "He got close enough to touch the gate. How is that even? possible?"

The officer replied, "He didn't breach the perimeter. He left the note on the outer fence. Cameras caught him, but he kept his face hidden."

"Coward," Devin muttered.

Alexis kept her eyes on the note but didn't open it again; she'd already read it. enough times.

Lex,

I'm not mad you ran. I will teach you the game. I knew you'd be smart enough to survive. But you took what's mine.

And I don't mean money.

You took the kids.

Bring them back, and everything goes back to normal. Or I come get them myself. Make the right choice.

; R.

The first message had been threatening. This one was a promise.

And Alexis felt something inside her harden into steel. "I'm not going back," she said firmly. "None of us are." Ms. Carter nodded. "Then we escalate. Today."

The security officer stepped forward. "We're moving you and your siblings to a fully confidential safe location; Level Three protection."

Devin frowned. "Level Three? That's the highest before witness protection."

"Correct," the officer confirmed. "We don't offer it often. But this man is persistent, and his criminal activity is documented. The department is taking this seriously."

Alexis swallowed. "What about my internship?"

"We'll arrange transportation," Ms. Carter said. "But we're not risking your safety."

Alexis nodded, but the heaviness in her chest lingered.

Rico wasn't stopping.

He was escalating.

The relocation van arrived an hour later. Blacked-out windows. A two-driver team. Bulletproof doors. Devin helped load the bags, his jaw clenched tight.

Mia clung to Alexis's side.

Jace kept asking questions.

Andre tried to act brave but stayed close to the security officer. Once they were settled, Ms. Carter pulled Alexis aside.

"He's trying to intimidate you," she said softly. "But remember; you're not that little girl anymore. You have support, you have rights, and you have a future he can't control."

Alexis nodded slowly. "I know."

"And one more thing," Ms. Carter added. "If he keeps pushing… we open a case. You won't have to hide forever."

The thought shook Alexis. Not hiding.

Fight.

Legally. Officially. For real.

As the van pulled away, Alexis watched the city blur past, buildings giving way to quieter streets. Devin followed in his car, refusing to be left behind.

The farther they drove, the more her heart pounded.

She wasn't afraid. Not exactly.

But she was done being hunted.

The new safehouse made the old one look like a motel. Tall fences. Security gates. Private apartments instead of dorm-style rooms. Cameras on every corner.

"Whoa," Andre whispered. "Are we famous now?" Alexis laughed weakly. "Something like that."

Inside, each child had a small room. A living room. A kitchen. A view of trees and a distant river.

Peace.

Real peace.

As they unpacked, a knock sounded at the door. Alexis opened it; and Rowan stood there, holding a wrapped box.

She blinked. "How did you even find this place?"

"I didn't," Rowan said quickly. "Security cleared the visit. I had to sign five forms."

Despite everything, she smiled. "You didn't have to come."

"Yeah," he replied gently, "I kind of did."

He glanced at the apartment. "This place is… impressive." "It has to be," Alexis murmured. "He found us again." Rowan's jaw tightened. "I'm sorry."

She shook her head. "Don't be. I'm done being scared."

He nodded slowly, then held out the box. "This is for you. It's… well, you'll see."

Alexis opened it carefully. Her breath caught.

Inside was a heavy-duty, professional-grade sketch tablet; bigger, sharper, and more advanced than anything she had ever used.

"It's not city property," Rowan added quickly, reading her expression. "It's from me. Personal gift. Completely separate from the internship."

Alexis ran her thumb across the smooth screen. "Why?"

"Because you're going to need the right tools," Rowan said softly. "Your project is spreading through the department. They're talking about using your design as a model for multiple neighborhoods. You're not just an intern anymore, Alexis."

Her heart thudded.

"You're a creator."

She looked up at him, eyes burning. "Thank you."

"You don't have to thank me," he said, voice low. "Just keep building. Don't let him take that from you."

For the first time in hours, Alexis breathed without tension.

That night, long after her siblings were asleep, Alexis sat at her new table by the window.

She opened a blank canvas.

Then, slowly, deliberately, she began drawing again. A neighborhood courtyard.

Wide spaces. Safe paths.

Light everywhere.

But this time, she added something new.

A gate. Strong. Unmovable.

Guarded.

A line, no one, especially Rico; would ever cross again.

Halfway through the drawing, her old phone buzzed in the drawer beside her. She froze.

She hadn't touched that phone since the night they ran.

The screen flashed with a single new message. Unknown number.

Her stomach dropped. She opened it.

"I know where you are."

Alexis's blood ran cold.

Not fear. Not panic.

Something sharper. Determination.

If Rico was coming…

Then so was her fight.

Chapter Twenty-Three
The Truth Behind the Threat

Alexis barely slept.

The message: I know where you are; echoed through her mind like a siren. She kept the old phone powered off, locked in a drawer, but the words burned behind her eyes. When dawn broke, she was already awake, already dressed, already pacing the small living room of the new safehouse apartment.

At seven sharp, Ms. Carter, the security officer, and Devin arrived for an emergency meeting.

Rowan wasn't allowed at the safehouse for this part; security protocol; but he'd already texted her:

Be strong. Whatever it is, we'll face it.

She clung to those words more than she wanted to admit.

The officer set a tablet on the table. "We traced the message."

Alexis froze.

"You did?" Devin asked, stepping closer.

"Yes. Rico used a prepaid phone. No GPS. But there was a single ping off a tower before it shut off."

The officer tapped the screen. "Location: the 12th District. A neighborhood you know well."

Alexis's stomach twisted. She knew exactly were.

His old block. His territory.

"But here's where things get complicated," the officer continued. "We also identified a second device near his location. Someone else is involved."

Alexis's eyes narrowed. "Who?" The officer hesitated. Too long. Ms. Carter answered instead. "Your mother."

Alexis felt the world tilt.

"My mother?" Her voice cracked, disbelief and anger colliding. "She's with him?"

"We can't confirm 'with,'" Ms. Carter clarified. "But the phone registered in the same vicinity within minutes of Rico's message."

Alexis shook her head, pacing away from the table. "No... no, she wouldn't. She wrote to me. She told me not to look for her."

"She also didn't tell you where she was," Devin said gently.

Alexis swallowed hard. Her throat felt thick and tight. "But why would she be near him? She hates him."

"People in addiction," Ms. Carter said softly, "don't always make choices based on hatred or love. Sometimes they make choices based on survival. Or pressure."

Alexis pressed a hand against her forehead. Was her mother helping Rico?

Was she being coerced?

91

Using him for drugs?

Or had she simply fallen back into the only world she knew? A cold wave of realization hit.

"Rico doesn't want us back because he cares about us," she whispered. "He wants control. He wants leverage."

Devin nodded. "He's never cared about them kids. Not once."

Ms. Carter folded her hands. "Which is why you need to hear this part clearly." The officer took over. "Rico recently came under investigation for trafficking." The room went dead silent.

Alexis's knees nearly buckled.

Devin cursed under his breath. "I knew that man was trash, but"

"We don't know the extent yet," the officer continued. "But he's being watched. He's getting desperate. And desperate people act erratically."

Alexis sank into the chair, her breathing uneven. Trafficking.

This wasn't just street business.

This was something darker.

Something that made her blood run cold.

"So, his message…" she whispered.

"Wasn't about wanting the kids," Ms. Carter confirmed. "It was about protecting.

himself. He fears you'll cooperate with authorities if they take him down."

The truth punched her in the chest.

Rico wasn't chasing her.

He was cornered; afraid she might expose him.

"I don't know anything," Alexis said quietly. "I never saw;"

"You saw enough," the officer replied. "Enough to place him around minors in unsafe conditions. Enough to describe his income, his behavior, his routines. And he knows that."

Alexis rubbed her eyes, her pulse thundering. "So, what do we do?"

"Protect you," Ms. Carter said firmly. "And build a legal case that keeps him away for good."

Devin leaned forward. "What do you need from Alexis?"

"We need a statement," the officer said. "A full, honest narrative of your experiences. Nothing exaggerated. Nothing hidden. Just the truth. And it needs to be soon."

Ms. Carter added, "You're not obligated. But if you choose to, it could help permanently sever Rico's reach."

Alexis swallowed. Her fingers curled into fists. This was the moment.

The line she'd been dancing around for years.

Running had kept her alive.

But fighting…

Fighting could finally free her. Still, the fear pulsed.

Giving a statement meant reopening wounds. Reliving everything she fought to leave behind. And what if Rico retaliated? Came harder? Tried again?

Devin touched her shoulder gently. "Lex. You won't be alone. Whatever you decide, I'm right here."

Ms. Carter nodded. "We'll increase your security. You'll be protected before, during, and after."

Alexis looked at the officer. "If I give the statement…, will it help keep him away from us? Legally?"

"It could lead to a protective order," the officer said. "Criminal charges. Possibly incarceration."

Alexis inhaled sharply. Finally.

Finally, an ending that didn't rely on running.

She closed her eyes for a moment.

Remember the nights she hid her siblings in closets. The times Rico slammed doors and broke things.

The fear. Hunger. The chaos.

The bruises she covered. The promises he broke.

And then she remembered her siblings' faces in the new safehouse.

Laughing. Eating.

Living without fear.

This wasn't just her fight.

It was theirs too.

She opened her eyes. Clear.

Steady.

Certain.

"I'll do it," she said. "I'll give the statement."

Ms. Carter nodded with deep respect. "We'll schedule it for tomorrow morning."

Devin let out a breath of relief. "Proud of you, Lex."

But the office wasn't finished.

"Before we end this meeting… there's one more thing you need to know." Alexis's tense. "What?"

He slid a manila folder across the table.

"Rico isn't just looking for you." Alexis's heartbeat stumbled.

"He's looking for your brother Andre."

The room spun.

"What? Why?" she demanded.

Ms. Carter answered gravely:

"Because Rico believes Andre already knows something that could destroy him."

And in that single moment, Alexis realized.

This fight was bigger, darker, and far more dangerous than she ever imagined.

Chapter Twenty-Four
What Andre Saw

Andre sat cross-legged on the carpet, building a lopsided tower out of plastic blocks, completely unaware that the adults in the next room were unraveling, the reason Rico wanted him back so badly.

Alexis watched him through the doorway, her heartbeat thudding like a drum under her ribs.

Her baby brothers. Only nine.

Small for his age.

Still afraid of the dark.

And somehow, he held a piece of a puzzle dangerous enough to make Rico hunt them.

Ms. Carter closed the door gently behind them. "Alexis, we need to ask Andre a few questions. But only with your consent."

Devin stepped closer, lowering his voice. "We don't have to push him if he's not ready."

Alexis swallowed, the fear clawing up her throat. "If Rico is after him... we don't have a choice."

The security officer nodded. "We'll proceed carefully."

The Gentle Approach

They moved to the living room. Alexis sat beside Andre while the officer sat on the floor across from him to avoid intimidating him.

"Andre," Alexis said softly, "these people need your help. Is that okay?" Andre shrugged. "Depends on what they ask."

Ms. Carter smiled. "Just want to talk, sweetheart."

The officer started slowly. "We've heard Rico was around the old apartment a lot before you left. Did you ever see him talking to strangers? Or acting weird?"

Andre pushed two blocks together, frowning.

"I saw him arguing a lot." "With whom?" Alexis asked.

Andre hesitated. "A man. I don't know his name." "Do you remember what he looked like?"

Andre nodded. "Tall. Mixed. Had a scar on his cheek. He came two times."

Alexis exchanged a sharp look with the adults. Scarred Cheek.

A name Devin muttered earlier; one of Rico's new guys.

"What were they arguing about?" the officer asked.

Andre's voice got quiet. "Rico said something like... 'you don't get paid until the package is moved.'"

The officer stiffened.

Ms. Carter gently asked, "What package, baby?"

96

Andre didn't answer immediately. Instead, he looked up at Alexis, conflicted, scared. "I'm not supposed to tell," he whispered.

Alexis's heart splintered. "Who told you that?"

Andre took too long to answer. When he finally did, his voice shook. "Rico."

The officer leaned forward. "Andre... what was the package?"

Andre's face crumpled with fear. "It wasn't a package. It was a girl."

Silence hit the room like a shockwave.

Alexis's throat dried. "A girl? What girl?"

"She was crying," Andre whispered. "She said she didn't want to go. Rico told me to shut up and go back upstairs, but I saw her. She had a purple backpack."

Alexis felt her stomach flip.

Ms. Carter's face had gone pale. "Andre... did the girl live in the building?" Andre shook his head. "No. I never saw her before."

The officer's voice grew tight. "Did she leave with them?"

Andre squeezed his eyes shut. "I don't know. I went upstairs. But I heard the door slam and a car drive off."

Alexis hugged him tightly, her entire body trembling.

Her little brother hadn't seen something. He'd seen evidence.

Real evidence.

Enough to connect Rico to trafficking.

This wasn't suspicion anymore.

This was a witness. A baby witness.

And Rico knew he saw it.

The Room Changes

The tone of the meeting shifted instantly. Firm.

Urgent. Strategic.

The officer stood. "This confirms our worst-case scenario. Rico's not after you for emotional reasons. He is trying to eliminate risk."

Devin cursed under his breath. "He's trying to cover his tracks."

Ms. Carter rubbed her temples. "We need to move fast. This is no longer just family conflict. This is criminal activity with a minor witness."

Alexis felt cold all over.

"What happens now?" she whispered.

The officer answered immediately:

"We open a joint case with the trafficking task force." "We schedule Andre for a protected forensic interview." "We lock down this safehouse to Level Three-plus."

"And Rico?" Alexis asked, her voice barely a breath.

The officer didn't sugarcoat it. "If he realizes Andre spoke out... he may escalate."

Alexis closed her eyes. Fear tried to rise.

I tried to choke her.

But something else rose too stronger. Resolve.

"This ends now," she said. "Whatever I have to do, I'm not letting him get near my family again."

Devin stepped beside her. "You're not doing it alone."

Ms. Carter nodded. "We'll handle the legal side. You focus on staying steady for your siblings."

And the officer added, "You giving your statement tomorrow is more important than ever."

Later That Night

After everyone left, Alexis tucked her siblings into bed. Andre held her hand tighter than usual.

"Lex?" he whispered. "Yeah?"

"Did I do something bad... seeing that girl?"

Alexis shook her head fiercely and kissed his forehead. "No, baby. You did something brave."

"Will she be okay?" he asked.

Alexis's chest tightened. She wished she knew.

"We're going to try," she said softly. "And your words can help."

He nodded, still scared, but calmer.

When he finally fell asleep, Alexis stepped into the kitchen and gripped the counter, her whole-body trembling.

Rico wasn't chasing them because of anger.

Or control.

Or pride.

He was chasing them because they held the truth.

A truth that could put him away forever.

And now Alexis knew:

She wasn't just saving her family anymore.

She was saving that girl with the purple backpack. And maybe others.

This fight had purpose.

This fight had weight.

This fight was survival for more than just her siblings.

Alexis wiped her face, straightened her shoulders, and whispered to herself:

"He should have never underestimated me."

Chapter Twenty-Five
The Day Everything Shakes

The next morning, the sky hung heavy with gray clouds; thick, swollen, ready to break.

Alexis felt the same.

Her statement was scheduled for nine a.m.

Andre's forensic interview at noon.

Security escorts waited outside the safehouse door.

It wasn't fear running down her spine now.

It was responsibility.

It was.

refused to let her family drown.

The Statement

The interview room inside the precinct was warmer than she expected. Soft lights. Neutral walls. A counselor sitting beside her, not across from her. Ms. Carter in the corner, calm but alert.

the weight of being the oldest. The protector.

The one who

The detective leading the interview, Detective Maris, had a kind but professional face.

"We'll go slow," she told Alexis. "You control the pace. You can stop or take breaks."

Alexis nodded, hands clapped together so tightly they trembled.

When the recorder clicked on, she took a breath that felt too big for her chest.

And she began.

She told them about the nights Rico disappeared and came home with money he didn't explain.

The girls she sometimes saw in the hallway, never the same ones twice. The arguments.

The threats.

The bruises she hides from school.

How he yelled at her mother until her mother broke.

How she protected her siblings. How she finally left.

She didn't exaggerate. She didn't embellish.

She told the truth.

Her voice shook only once; when she spoke about the night she ran with her siblings, how she held their hands so tight their fingers went numb.

Detective Maris didn't interrupt. didn't rush her.

Just listened, eyes steady, pen still.

When Alexis finished, she felt hollowed out; like she'd poured her whole chest onto the table.

"So," she whispered, "what happens now?"

Detective Maris paused the recorder. "Now? We build the case. And we protect your family."

Alexis nodded, tears burning her eyes, but she didn't let them fall. She'd done her part.

Next was Andre.

Andre's Turn

Forensic interviews for kids were different.

A child specialist met him in a separate room filled with toys, soft chairs, gentle colors. Alexis watched through a one-way window with Ms. Carter and the detective. Andre looked so small on that couch. Feet dangling.

Hands twisting in his lap.

But when the specialist asked him about the girl with the purple backpack, he spoke clearly.

Quietly. But clearly.

Alexis wiped her eyes silently.

Her brother: brave in ways a child should never have to be. The interview lasted forty minutes.

When Andre came out, he ran straight to Alexis.

"Was I okay?" he asked.

She hugged him tightly. "You were perfect."

A Dangerous Shift

As they prepared to leave the precinct, Detective Maris pulled Ms. Carter aside.

"We got a ping," she said. "Rico's phone. Near Delaney Park." Ms. Carter frowned. "That's too close to the old safehouse." Alexis overheard, heart stopping. "What does that mean?" "It means," Detective Maris said, "he's scouting."

The air in the hallway thickened.

Devin stepped closer instinctively. "Is he looking for them again?"

"Most likely," she admitted. "We're increasing patrols around the new safehouse, but we need to keep your moving. Safe, not predictable."

The plan was to transport them back in the same security van. But when they stepped outside, the officer escorting them suddenly froze.

"Get back inside," he barked.

Alexis's pulse spiked. "What's happening?"

102

He lifted his radio. "We've got a vehicle matching the description across the street."
A black sedan with tinted windows sat at the curb. Engine running.
Silent. Waiting.
Alexis's stomach dropped.
Before panic could rise, Devon moved in front of her and the kids, shielding them. "Is it him?" he demanded.
"We don't know yet," the officer answered, hand on his holster. "We're not taking chances. Stay behind the glass."
Alexis pulled Andre close. Jace and Mia clung to her sides.
The sedan didn't move. Didn't roll down a window. Didn't show a face.
Just idle.
A threat without saying a word.
Detective Maris radioed backup, her voice sharp. "Do not engage. Do not approach. Units end route."
Seconds stretched into forever. Then.
The sedan's tires screeched.
It sped off.
Rounded the corner. Gone.
Leaving exhaust. Leaving questions.
Leaving dread in its wake.

The Calm After the Threat

They waited ten tense minutes before being escorted underground to a reinforced garage.
Two cars followed them back to the safehouse. Security monitored every entrance.
Inside the apartment, the kids clumped together on the couch, shaken. Alexis stepped into the bedroom, Devin following quietly.
Her hands shook uncontrollably.
"He was there," she whispered. "He was really there." "We don't know it was him;" Devin began.
"Who else watches a precinct?" she snapped, voice breaking.
Devin softened instantly. "Lex… he's scared. Angry. But we're not playing defense anymore. You gave a statement. Andre gave him. He's losing control."
She pressed her hand to her forehead. "And that makes him dangerous."
"It also makes him sloppy," Devin countered. "And sloppy people get caught."
Alexis sank into bed. "I'm so tired."
Devin sat beside her, gentle. "I know." "I don't want to keep running."
"You won't have to," he promised. "We're close. I can feel it."

She looked up at him, eyes glassy. "Everything's happening so fast."

Devin reached for her hand; firm, grounding; but she pulled away gently.

Not because she didn't want comfort.

But because something inside her was changing.

There wasn't room in her chest for romance.

Not yet.

Maybe not for a long time.

Right now, she needed strength. Focus.

Control.

She drew a shaky breath. "I just need space to think." Devin nodded without offense. "I get it."

He stood and left her to breathe.

A Quiet Resolve

That night, long after the kids fell asleep, Alexis sat by the window with her sketch tablet, Rowan's gift.

She didn't draw buildings.

Or courtyards. Or blueprints.

She drew the black sedan. Every curve.

Every angle.

Every detail she remembered.

And when she was finished, she added something to the background: Police lights.

Flashing. Bright.

Closing in.

When she set the tablet down, she whispered to herself:

"He won't win this time. Not this time." Her fear hadn't vanished.

But something stronger had taken its place.

Purpose. Rage.

Courage.

And in the dark outside, headlights flashed briefly. A shadow passed the fence line.

Alexis didn't flinch.

Let him come.

She wasn't the hunted girl anymore.

She was the storm building on the horizon.

Chapter Twenty-Six
When the Net Tightens

The call came just before dawn.

Alexis was half-awake, curled on the couch with a blanket, when Ms. Carter's name lit up her phone. Her stomach tightened instantly.

"Ms. Carter?"

"Alexis, listen carefully," she said, voice low and urgent. "The task force is moving on

Rico this morning."

Alexis sat straight up. "Moving how?"

"They've got enough probable cause for coordinated raids. Multiple locations. But we don't know if he's going to be where they expect."

Alexis's pulse raced. "So, this is it?"

"It's the beginning," Ms. Carter replied. "But it's the most dangerous part."

The Waiting

Security protocol went into full lockdown.

Blinds closed.

Phones monitored.

No one in or out.

The kids sensed the tension immediately.

"Why can't we go to school?" Mia asked, hugging her backpack.

Alexis knelt in front of her. "Just a safety day, baby. Movie day at home."

Andre didn't ask questions. He stayed close, quiet, eyes too observant for his age.

As the hours dragged, Alexis paced the apartment, refreshing the news on mute, heart pounding with every passing minute.

Somewhere in the city, officers were kicking down doors.

Searching rooms.

Calling names.

And Rico was either about to be caught-

Or about to run.

The Mistake

At 10:47 a.m., Alexis's phone buzzed with an unknown number.

Her blood ran cold.

Devin noticed immediately. "Don't answer that."

"I won't," she said-then froze when a second buzz followed.

A text message appeared.

Unknown: Your brother told the truth. Now look what you started.

Alexis's breath caught.

Before she could think, another message came through.

Unknown: You think they can protect you forever?

Her hands shook violently.

Devin grabbed her phone. "This is bait."

"I know," she whispered.

But then-

A third message.

Unknown: Your mama's hurt.

The room spun.

Alexis lurched to her feet. "What?"

Devin's grip tightened. "Lex-don't."

"What if it's true?" she cried. "What if he-"

Before reason could stop her, Alexis typed back.

Alexis: Where is she?

The moment she hit send; regret slammed into her chest.

Devin swore. "Damn it."

Ms. Carter's voice rang in Alexis's Head-Don't engage.

The phone buzzed again immediately.

Unknown: You still care. Meet me.

Alexis felt sick.

Devin took the phone, reading quickly. "We need to give this to the task force. Right now."

"But my mother-"

"We don't know if she's actually hurt," Devin said firmly. "And even if she is, this is

how he pulls you out."

Alexis collapsed onto the couch, shaking. "I just wanted to know."

Devin softened. "I know. But this... this could get you killed."

The Trap Revealed

Within minutes, Detective Maris and two officers were on a secure video call.

"You did the right thing telling us," Maris said, though her eyes were sharp. "We believe Rico sent that message while on the move."

"Can you track him?" Alexis asked.

"We're trying," Maris replied. "But prepaid phones are tricky."

Ms. Carter joined the call. "Alexis, you must not respond again. Do you understand?"

Alexis nodded, tears streaking down her face. "Yes."

Maris leaned closer to the camera. "I need you to hear this clearly. Rico is losing everything today. That makes him unpredictable. He may try to force a face-to-face."

Alexis swallowed hard. "He already is."

There was a pause.

Then Maris said, "If he reaches out again, we want him talking. Not to you-but through us."

"What does that mean?" Alexis asked.

"It means," Maris replied carefully, "we may need to use you as leverage."

The words landed heavy.

Devin stiffened. "Absolutely not."

Ms. Carter raised a hand. "Only if Alexis consents. And only with full protection."

Alexis stared at the floor.

Leverage.

A word that tasted like danger.

But also, like control.

If Rico was desperate enough to reach out...

Maybe that desperation could be turned against him.

The Choice

Another text buzzed.

Unknown: Last chance.

Alexis looked up slowly.

"He's pushing," she said.

Devin shook his head. "Lex, no."

Ms. Carter spoke gently. "This is your choice."

Alexis's heart hammered so hard she felt dizzy.

She thought of Andre.

Of the girl with the purple backpack.

Of every night she hid in fear.

If she did nothing, Rico might vanish.

If she acted, he might finally be caught.

She took a breath so deep it hurt.

"I'll help," she said quietly. "But I won't meet him. Not alone."

Detective Maris nodded. "Agreed. We'll control the situation."

Devin grabbed her hand. "You don't have to do this."

Alexis squeezed back, tears burning. "I know. But I can't let him keep hurting people."

Maris said, "We'll draft the message. You'll send it. Then we wait."

Alexis's fingers hovered over the screen as the detective dictated:

Alexis: If my mother's hurt, I need to see her. Talk to me. No games.

Her hand trembled as she sent it.

Seconds passed.

Then the reply came.

Unknown: Tonight. Come alone.

Alexis's chest tightened.

Maris spoke calmly, decisively.

"He wants a meeting."

Devin whispered fiercely, "No."

Alexis looked at the screen, then at the faces around her.

"He won't get me," she said softly. "But he will show himself."

And somewhere across the city, Rico believed he still held the power-

Not knowing the net had already closed around him.

Chapter Twenty-Seven
Face to Face

The plan was simple.

Which meant it was dangerous.

Alexis would not go anywhere near Rico; but he would believe she was on her way. The task force would monitor every message, every move, every shadow. Unmarked cars would surround the meeting location long before he arrived.

If Rico showed his face…

They would take him.

Alexis sat in a secure operations room at the precinct, surrounded by quiet urgency. Screens glowed with maps and live camera feeds. Officers spoke in clipped whispers. Detective Maris stood at the center, calm and commanding.

"You won't leave this room," Maris told Alexis firmly. "Your phone is the hook. That's it."

Alexis nodded, jaw tight. "I understand."

Devin stood behind her chair, arms crossed, tension radiating off him. Rowan wasn't allowed in the room; but he'd texted once, earlier:

Whatever happens tonight, remember who you are.

She held onto that.

The Bait

At 7:14 p.m., Alexis's phone buzzed.

Unknown: Delaney Warehouse. Back entrance. 9 p.m.

Detective Maris zoomed in on the map. "That place has been on our radar for months."

Ms. Carter murmured, "He's sloppy. Or he's desperate." "Or both," Maris replied.

Alexis swallowed. "What about my mother?"

Maris met her eyes. "We believe he's lying. But we have teams searching nearby shelters and clinics just in case.

The words stung; but Alexis nodded. She typed the response Maris dictated. Alexis: I'll be there.

The lie sat heavy in her chest.

The Wait

The hours crawled.

At 8:45, officers moved in. Drones hovered. Plainclothes units slipped into alleyways. Surveillance cameras flickered to life on the monitors.

Alexis watched the warehouse feed, pulse roaring in her ears. 9:00 p.m.

Nothing. 9:06.

A black sedan rolled into frames.

Alexis's breath caught.

"Vehicle matches prior sightings," an officer said quietly.

The car was idle.

A man stepped out. Tall.

Broad.

Familiar in a way that made Alexis's skin crawl.

Rico.

He looked older. Rougher.

But his posture, the way he scanned the shadows like he owned them, hadn't changed.

Alexis's stomach twisted. "That's him," she whispered.

Rico paced near the entrance, phone in hand.

Unknown: I'm here. Where are you?

Maris nodded. "Respond."

Alexis: Running late. Don't leave.

Rico cursed aloud, the audio feeding picking it up. He kicked a loose crate, anger flashing across his face.

"Teams, hold," Maris ordered. "Wait for confirmation." Rico stepped deeper into the alley, checking behind him. Then he spoke.

Not on the phone. Out loud.

"You really thought I wouldn't see through you?" Alexis's heart slammed.

On the monitor, Rico looked straight up, directly at a security camera.

"You always were smart," he said, voice low and sharp. "But not smarter than me."

The room froze.

"He knows," Devin muttered.

Maris didn't flinch. "He suspects. Doesn't mean he knows everything."

Rico raised his phone again.

Unknown: I know you're not coming. But I came anyway.

Alexis's throat tightened.

Why?

The Turn

Rico reached into his jacket.

Officers tense.

But instead of a weapon, he pulled out another phone and tossed it into the alley.

Then he smiled.

And that smile was wrong.

"Something's off," an officer said.

Before Maris could respond, Rico's phone buzzed again.

Not from Alexis. From someone else.

His expression changed, panic flashing across his face. He bolted.

"Go! Go! Go!" Maris shouted.

Officers surged into motion. The warehouse exploded with flashing lights. Sirens screamed. Rico ran; fast, desperate; cutting between dumpsters and crates.

Alexis stood frozen, watching chaos unfold on the screen.

"Foot pursuit!" someone yelled.

Rico vaulted a fence, disappearing from one camera.

Then reappearing on another, cornered at the edge of the loading dock. Two officers closed in.

Rico spun, raised hands; then lunged. A struggle.

A shout.

Metal clattered to the ground.

"Suspect restrained!" an officer yelled.

Alexis's knees buckled as Devin caught her.

On-screen, Rico was slammed face-first onto the concrete, wrists cuffed behind his back. His face twisted with fury as officers read him his rights.

But even then; Even pinned.

He lifted his head and spoke.

"You think this is over?" he snarled. "You think she won?" Maris leaned into the mic. "Yes."

Rico laughed bitterly. "Then you don't know what she gave up." Alexis's breath caught.

"What does that mean?" she whispered.

The Aftermath

Rico was loaded into the cruiser.

The warehouse fell silent except for radios crackling and officers catching their breath.

But the victory felt... incomplete.

Maris turned to Alexis. "We have him. Multiple charges. Trafficking. Witness intimidation. Child endangerment."

Alexis exhaled shakily.

"He's done," Devin said softly.

But Alexis couldn't shake Rico's last words.

You don't know what she gave up.

"What did he mean?" she asked.

Maris's face tightened. "We're still investigating."

Ms. Carter stepped closer. "Alexis… there's one more thing."

Alexis looked up, dread curling in her chest.

"We located your mother."

Alexis's heart leapt. "Where is she?"

Ms. Carter hesitated.

"In custody," she said gently. "Protective custody." Alexis's breath stuttered.

"For what?" she whispered.

Ms. Carter met her eyes and voice heavy.

"For cooperating with Rico."

The words crashed down on her. Not just trapped.

Not just addicted.

Her mother had been helping him. The room blurred.

Rico was in cuffs.

But the damage he'd done.

It was deeper than prison bars.

And Alexis realized the final battle wouldn't be in the streets…

It would be in her heart.

Chapter Twenty-Eight
After the Sirens Fade

The city didn't stop just because Rico was in handcuffs.

Traffic still moved.

Buses still ran late.

People still hurried past one another, unaware that somewhere behind concrete walls, a storm had finally broken.

For Alexis, the silence after the sirens was the loudest sound, she had ever known.

The Visit

Protective custody felt nothing like protection.

The room was beige and cold, a metal table bolted to the floor, two chairs facing each other like a confrontation neither woman had prepared for.

Alexis sat first.

When her mother was escorted in, Alexis barely recognized her.

Serena was thinner. Hollowed out. Her eyes darted around the room like she was still looking for a way to disappear.

"Lex..." her mother whispered.

Alexis didn't answer.

Minutes passed.

Finally, Alexis spoke. "You helped him."

Serena flinched. "I didn't have a choice."

"You always say that," Alexis replied, her voice steady but tight. "You had a choice when he hurt us. When he used the house. When Andre saw that girl."

Serena's eyes filled with tears. "You don't understand how deep it goes."

Alexis leaned forward. "I understand addiction. I understand fear. What I don't understand is choosing him over your kids."

Serena covered her face, sobbing quietly.

"I was scared," she said. "He said he'd take the kids if I talked. He said you were going to ruin everything."

Alexis's chest ached. "You ruined it when you stayed silent."

Serena looked up, desperation etched into her face. "Can you forgive me?"

The question hung heavy.

Alexis thought of all the nights she became a parent instead of a child.

Of the fear Andre carried.

Of the girl with the purple backpack.

"I don't know," Alexis said honestly. "Forgiveness isn't a switch. It's work."

Serena nodded, broken. "I'll do anything."

Alexis stood. "Then start by staying away from us until you're clean. Until you're safe."

Tears streamed down Serena's face. "I love you."

Alexis paused at the door. "I believe you. But love isn't enough."

And for the first time in her life, Alexis walked away without guilt.

Breaking Ground

Two weeks later, the fence went up.

Alexis stood beside Rowan at the construction site, hard hat perched awkwardly on her head, boots still a little too new.

"This is it," Rowan said, smiling. "Your design. Your vision."

The old lot-once cracked concrete and trash-was alive with movement. Workers measured, dug, marked boundaries.

Alexis watched in awe as her drawings became reality.

"Courtyard housing," Rowan explained to a group of city officials. "Community-centered, light-focused, affordable. Designed by Alexis Grant."

Hearing her name said like that-without pity, without hesitation-made her chest swell.

After the meeting, Rowan turned to her. "You're officially being brought on as a paid

junior designer."

Alexis blinked. "You're serious?"

"Very," he said. "You earned this."

She laughed softly, tears in her eyes. "I used to draw this stuff in notebooks so no one would laugh at me."

Rowan smiled. "Now they're building it."

Healing Looks Like This

The kids started therapy.

Andre slept through the night again.

Mia joined an art club.

Jace stopped flinching at loud noises.

They moved into transitional housing-clean, bright, stable.

Alexis cooked real meals. Helped with homework. Watched movies without checking the door every five minutes.

One night, as she tucked Andre in, he whispered, "Is he gone forever?"

Alexis smoothed his hair. "He can't hurt us anymore."

Andre nodded, finally peaceful.

Letting Herself Breathe

On a quiet evening, Alexis sat on the balcony of their new place, city lights twinkling in the distance.

Devin leaned against the railing beside her.

"You did it," he said softly.

"We did it," she corrected.

He smiled. "You still carrying everything on your shoulders?"

She considered the question.

"Not everything," she said. "I'm learning what I can put down."

Devin nodded, respecting the space between them. "Whenever you're ready... I'll be here."

She appreciated that more than he knew.

A Different Kind of Strength

Later, Alexis opened her sketch tablet.

This time, she didn't draw gates or police lights.

She drew people.

Children playing in a courtyard.

Neighbors talking.

Light spilling into shared spaces.

A future that didn't revolve around fear.

Alexis smiled softly.

Rico was behind bars.

Her mother was facing her choices.

Her siblings were healing.

And for the first time, Alexis allowed herself to believe:

Survival was over.

Now came the rise.

Chapter Twenty-Nine
The Moment Before the Rise

The courtyard opened on a Saturday morning.

Sunlight poured into the space like it had been waiting its turn.

Alexis stood at the edge of the lot, hands tucked into the pockets of her blazer, watching families drift in; some curious, some cautious, all hopefuls. The concrete that once held nothing, but trash and broken glass had transformed into warm walkways, garden beds, benches, and wide-open breathing room.

Her design.

Her proof.

Rowan approached, clipboard in hand. "You ready?" She smiled faintly. "I think so."

"You should know," he added, lowering his voice, "this project is being looked at by the regional housing board."

Alexis blinked. "Looked at how?"

"As a model," Rowan said. "They're considering adapting it in three other neighborhoods."

Her heart skipped.

Before she could respond, a city councilwoman stepped up to the microphone.

"Today," the woman announced, "we don't just open a courtyard. We open possibility."

Applause rippled through the crowd.

Alexis felt a strange mix of pride and disbelief. Just months ago, she'd been hiding from the world. Now the world was standing inside something she created.

The Unexpected Visit

As the ribbon was wrapped up, Alexis drifted toward the garden beds, running her fingers over fresh soil. Children laughed nearby. A neighbor waved at her like they'd known each other forever.

Then she felt it.

That familiar tightening in her chest. She turned slowly.

A woman stood near the entrance, flanked by a caseworker. Serena.

Her mother looked healthier than the last time Alexis saw her. Still fragile; but sober. Present.

Alexis's heart pounded.

Rowan noticed her stillness. "You want me to;" "No," Alexis said quietly. "I've got this."

She approached cautiously.

Serena didn't step forward. "I didn't know if you'd want me here." Alexis crossed her arms. "Why did you come?"

"To see you," Serena said honestly. "And to say… I pled guilty."

The words hit Alexis harder than she expected.

"What?"

"I told them everything," Serena continued. "About Rico. About girls. About the money. I'm entering treatment as part of the deal."

Alexis searched her face for lies; and found none.

"That doesn't erase anything," Alexis said.

"I know," Serena replied, eyes wet. "But it's a start."

They stood in silence, the sound of children filling the space between them.

Serena gestured weakly to the courtyard. "You built this." Alexis nodded. "I did."

Serena smiled sadly. "You always were stronger than me."

Alexis inhaled deeply. "Strength isn't doing it alone. It's choosing better; every day."

Serena nodded. "I'm trying."

Alexis held her gaze. "Trying is good. Consistency is better." Serena swallowed.

"May I… be part of your life again someday?" Alexis didn't answer right away.

Finally, she said, "Maybe. After time. After proof." Serena nodded, accepting the boundary. "That's fair."

As Serena walked away with the case worker, Alexis felt something loosen inside her chest.

Not forgiveness. But possibility.

Recognition

Later, a man in a tailored suit introduced himself as a representative from an architecture scholarship foundation.

"We've been following your work," he said. "Your background, your design philosophy; it's compelling."

He handed her a card. "We'd like you to apply. Full funding."

Alexis stared at it, stunned.

Rowan beamed. "Told you."

Across the courtyard, her siblings waved.

Andre held up a drawing he'd made; four stick figures inside a big square, smiling.

Mia whispered something to Jace, and they both laughed.

This was it. Not the end.

But the beginning of a life where fear didn't get the final word.

The Last Test

As the crowd thinned, Detective Maris approached.

"Everything okay?" Alexis asked.

Maris nodded. "Rico accepted a plea deal. Twenty-five years. No parole for a long time."

Alexis closed her eyes briefly. Gone.

Maris continued, "He asked about you." Alexis opened her eyes. "And?"

"I told him you were busy building something he could never touch."

Alexis smiled.

Standing in the Light

As the sun dipped low, Alexis stood in the center of the courtyard alone. She thought of the girl she once was hungry, afraid, determined.

She whispered softly, "We made it."

The city hummed around her.

And somewhere deep inside, a new chapter waited; One without running.

One without shadows. Just before the rise.

Chapter Thirty
She Rose!

One year later, the courtyard was alive.

Not with ceremony this time; but with life.

Children chased each other across warm stone paths. Elders sat on benches shaded by young trees. Music drifted softly from an open window somewhere above. The buildings stood strong and welcoming, curved just enough to feel human, just enough to feel safe.

Alexis Grant stood near the center, hands folded, watching it all.

She wore confidence the way she once wore armor; quietly, naturally, without needing to announce it.

A banner fluttered near the entrance:

GRANT COURTYARD: A COMMUNITY-BUILT SPACE

Her last name. Her legacy.

The Speech

The microphone felt lighter than she expected.

Alexis looked out at the crowd; neighbors, city officials, workers, teachers, and kids who now live here. Her siblings sat in the front row, eyes shining.

Andre gave her a thumb-up. She smiled.

"I used to believe survival was the goal," Alexis began. "That if you made it through the night, which was enough."

The crowd fell silent.

"I grew up thinking the world had already decided who I would be. Poor. Invisible. Broken before I ever had a chance."

She paused, steadily.

"But survival isn't living. And fear isn't destiny."

She gestured around her.

"This courtyard exists because someone once told me I didn't belong anywhere else; and I decided to prove them wrong. Not with anger. Not with revenge. But with vision."

Applause rippled through the crowd.

"I built this for families like mine. For kids who deserve sunlight instead of sirens. For people who want safety without shame."

Her voice caught; but she held it.

"And for anyone who thinks their past disqualifies them from a future; I'm standing here to tell you it doesn't."

She stepped back from the microphone. The applause rose, long and loud.

Full Circle

Later, Alexis walked through the courtyard with her siblings.

Mia pointed to a mural. "That's my favorite part." Jace said, "This place smells like plants, not trash."

Andre stayed close, but he smiled easily now. "I like that nobody's yelling."

Alexis knelt, meeting their eyes. "This is home. And no one can take it from us."

They hugged her all at once.

Quiet Wins

That evening, Alexis sat at her desk in her apartment overlooking the courtyard.

Acceptance letters lay open.

A full architecture scholarship. A long-term design contract.

A future that stretched wide instead of closing in. Her phone buzzed.

A message from Rowan:

Proud of you. Always.

She smiled, then set the phone down.

Some connections didn't need labels yet.

Some things could grow slowly; like everything worth keeping.

The Past at Rest

Across town, behind concrete walls and locked doors, Rico watched the news replay silently.

Alexis Grant. Her name.

Her work.

He turned away.

For the first time in his life, he had no power left to reach her.

The Future, Claimed

That night, Alexis returned to the courtyard alone. The lights glowed softly.

Footsteps echoed gently.

Life hummed.

She stood where fear once lived; and breathed.

"I'm not running anymore," she whispered.

The city answered with quiet acceptance.

Alexis Grant had risen; not by escaping her past, but by outgrowing it.

And from the concrete she was born into...

She built something unbreakable.

THE END